ANGELS AT WAR

SAMANTHA JACOBEY

Lavish
Publishing LLC

First Edition

Summer Spirit Series, book 1

All Rights Reserved

Published in the United States by Lavish Publishing, LLC, Midland, Texas

Cover Design by: Victor R. Sosa

Cover Images: Canstock

Paperback Edition

ISBN: 978-1-64900-090-3

www.LavishPublishing.com

Contents

Part III

Forgotten Angel

Angels at War

Summer Spirit Series book 1

For Steven; dream big, my Angel

PART I
Summer Angel

Prologue

"LET's GO, CHARLIE!" Bethany Phillips hollered up the stairs, "We're gonna miss our flight!"

"I'm comin', I'm comin'!" her eighteen-year-old son called back at her, "I gotta get all my stuff."

"Relax, Beth," her husband soothed. "We got plenty o' time. It's our last vacation with him under our roof, so le's enjoy it, ok?"

"Sure, John," she grimaced, "As soon as we land in Miami, I'll start enjoyin' it." Fidgeting, she turned her back on the man, aware that they never saw eye to eye these days.

Shaking his head, the older man helped his son haul his suitcases out to the awaiting van. Giving the boy a pleading glance, he yearned for peace between the pair; *I hope she knows how important this is to me. My last summer to spend with my son before he really becomes a man.*

"I don' know why we have to take a whole two weeks of vacation, anyways," Charlie complained while he strapped himself in. "Yeah, I'm goin' t' college, but I'm gonna be in Austin, for Christ's sakes! It's only a couple o' hours from here."

"That's not the point," his mother explained for the umpteenth time. "The point is, nothin'll be the same after you leave. An' we wanna enjoy you bein' our little man, just one more time. So, humor me, 'k?"

Exhaling loudly through his nostrils, Charles Phillips stared out the window. Watching the east Texas terrain flying by, he could see his brown waves reflected in the glass. Reaching up to tap them, his mahogany orbs drooped at all that he would miss with his friends.

Pulling out his cellphone, he checked in on Facebook, looking over a few of their posts, and what was going on in his world. Heaving another heavy sigh, he shoved the device back in his pocket to glare at the scenery again. Before long they would be in San Antonio, and boarding their flight, off to the summer cottage that would house them for their two week stay in Florida.

In reality, the bungalow belonged to his aunt Belinda; *mom's twin sister,* he recalled. But, she had insisted on their taking it for the trip, knowing how badly they wanted to go. *Fine,* he pouted, hunkering down in his seat a little further. *I guess I can play along. But if they think I'll ever go on another stupid trip with them after this, they can dream on!*

Unloading in front of the entrance, his father placed the bags on the curb and instructed them to wait while he parked the vehicle. Standing in the warm Texas heat, Charlie noticed a tall blonde in a straw hat observing him coyly from the corner of her eye. Breaking into a wide grin, he gave the girl a nod, which only earned him the faintest of smiles. *Damn, she's pretty,* he observed her pale blue eyes and creamy porcelain skin, before his mother interrupted his train of thought.

"Grab th' bags son; we need to hustle if we're gonna make it," she implored, continuing on in a cascade of instructions and complaints.

"Yes, ma'am," he did his best to comply. Lifting one pack onto his shoulder and rolling the other, Charlie trailed along behind, trying to keep up while scanning the crowd. *Man, that sucks; catch sight of just the kind o' girl I'd like to meet, when I have no chance of it happening.*

ONE

Fine as Silk

"EARTH TO CHARLIE!" Clarisse called again, waving her hand in front of the young man's face. "Hello! Anybody home?"

"What?" his brown eyes blinked rapidly against the glare. Noticing the crowd pushing and milling around them, he took a step back, staring at the fair-haired girl working to garner his attention, "Who are you?"

"Who am I?" she stammered, her crystal blue orbs displaying genuine anguish. "I'm Clarisse," she stamped her foot slightly, pulling her hands to her hips in the form of fists. "We met this morning? You can't have forgotten."

He stared at the blond whiffs of hair, noting they were as fine as silk, floating slightly in the gentle breeze. Pretending recognition, he agreed, "Oh, yeah. So what're we gonna do next?" He posed the query, hoping it would come off as appropriate; *I have no clue who this girl is!*

Giving him a slow smile, she nodded, "This way." Catching his hand, she entwined their fingers, swinging them whimsically while leading him down the walk.

Stealing a sideways glance at the corner, Charlie observed that she wore white shorts, with a white tank top. Most of her flesh exposed, he could see she probably did not dress so scantily under normal conditions, and her skin would qualify as ghost white.

Her cotton-blond locks were long and straight, parted in the middle of her forehead, and hanging almost to the hem of her shorts. Matching his six foot frame within an inch or two, she appeared tall and lanky. The sun surrounding her, the paleness of her being almost gave her an ethereal glow in the bright light.

"So, finish telling me about your school," she cajoled playfully when they entered a small cafe and scooted into matching tan seats, facing one another.

"My school," he faltered, unsure which school she referred to, or what he might have already said. "There really isn't much else to tell. Why don't you tell me about yours," he tried to weasel his way out. He pulled a menu out of the holder next to the window and gave it a frown, "Nothing looks good."

"It's ok, we don't have to eat yet. It was only a suggestion," she smiled at him, her lips perfectly turned, stunningly beautiful.

"Ok," he nodded, "We can try again later." Standing, they made their way outside, where they moved slowly, his nerves beginning to relax after the initial shock. Noticing she studied him intently, he grinned sheepishly, "So, care to tell me about yourself?"

"I'm from Maine," she supplied with a small grin, "Originally," her tongue flitted across her lips in a quick circle, "But lately I'm all over. I never stay in one place for very long." She produced a pair of sunglasses, almost clear with a soft blue tint, and dropped them onto her face casually.

"You already finished school then?"

"Something like that," she looked away, appearing slightly nervous. "Oh, I have to take this," she exclaimed, opening her hand where a small cellphone in a white case appeared. Sliding her finger over the screen, she glared at it for a long moment, making choices of what looked to be icons, followed by a brief video. Closing her hand a moment later, the device disappeared.

"Everything ok?" he smiled, having noticed the strain flitter across her features.

"All fine," she smiled brightly again. "Many people depend on me, Charlie. It's my job, I guess you could say."

"The one that means you travel," he casually dropped his gaze to her perfect little rear end when she turned to look for the bus. *Where's the phone?* He observed her pockets were empty, her outfit too tight against her slender frame for hiding places. "So what is it that you do, exactly?" he asked, sinking into his seat on the massive transport a moment later.

"I'm a consultant of sorts," she flicked her hair and dusted imaginary dirt off of her pristine clothing. "I help people avoid unpleasant or harmful situations."

"Oh, that sounds really cool!" he grinned, taking in the front side of her, not locating the rectangle that would indicate her hidden apparatus.

Bumping along in silence for several minutes, he only felt mildly curious where she was taking him. Somehow, being in her presence, he didn't feel concerned about anything else. Not rushed, or irritated in any way, almost as if nothing else mattered. "So, how do you get your clients?"

"Oh," she paused, her soft grey orbs appearing distant, the glasses no longer covering them, "They sometimes come to me. Others, my boss messages me to take them on. And of course, I do what I can, either way." Adjusting herself to sit up straighter, her voice dropped almost to a whisper, "Do you believe in magic, Charlie?"

"Magic?" he scoffed, "That depends. Are you talking about in books or movies, or regular stuff?"

"Well, regular stuff I guess."

"Then no, I don't believe in magic. There's no realistic basis for it."

She giggled loudly, "What if I could make you believe, Charlie?"

He stared at her with wide brown eyes, his mouth suddenly dry, "How're you gonna do that?" he demanded almost angrily; *what in the hell is going on with this girl?*

"Relax, Charlie, I'm not going to hurt you! I only want to let you in… on my secret," her face turned down, she cut her eyes up at him.

Returning his gaze to the front of the bus, he stretched his neck until it cracked quietly. *Great, I meet a pretty girl I'd like to know better, and BAM… she's loony-toons.* First, she claimed to know him, when he had never seen her before in his life. *Wait. I have seen her before!* Stealing a look out of the corner of his eye, he finally recognized her. *She was at the airport before we left Texas.* He was sure of it.

Rubbing the outside of his lips with anxious fingers, he glanced to the left, at the people next to him, who seemed oblivious to the couple's presence. *And now she wants to prove to me that magic exists.* Feeling as if he should be somewhere else; like his mother or father would be looking for him, he sighed deeply. "I think I need to get back to my parents."

"Your parents are fine, Charlie. They know where you are, remember?" She smiled sweetly, "It will only take a few hours, I promise. Let me prove it to you, so you can believe, and then you can return to your family, if you wish."

No, I don't remember, he challenged her silently, raking his jaw side to side. Meeting her gaze, he stared into the crystal blue orbs, feeling himself being drawn in. "Ok, Clarisse," he bobbed his head lightly. "Of course, this should be interesting to see. I'm pretty confident, here, an' I doubt you're gonna change that."

The girl grinned, returning her glasses to her face and staring straight ahead as they bumped along on the cushioned seats.

TWO

Rules of Magic

STANDING when the bus came to a halt, Clarisse showed him her perfect white teeth, "That wasn't so hard." She guided him off with a soft touch on his elbow, and led him towards the sidewalk and onto a beach. "The first thing we need to go over are the rules of magic. There are only a few, but they are very important."

The young man grinned from ear to ear, as if he were already on to her game, "Rules, huh," he rubbed his palms together eagerly, "I can't wait to hear this."

"The first rule," she remained calm, "Is that only those who are chosen can see it, even if they experience it. If they're not part of the chosen, they ignore it."

"So everyone has magic in their life, they just don't know it."

"Absolutely," she nodded, her hair blowing gently in the breeze, "There is magic all around us. It comes from another dimension, one that living people cannot see." Turning, she slipped off her shoes and took a seat on the soft, warm earth beneath them.

"And why don't they see it?" he inquired, dropping onto the ground next to her, noticing that her naked toes curled into the sand. Removing his shoes to join her, he sat with bare feet pressed into the warm grains as well.

"Because it's against the rules," she appeared wistful for a moment, "The universe has its divisions; its laws of physics if you will. Man struggles to understand them, and sometimes even to break them. But they are unbreakable, Charlie. They must be followed, and we can do no other."

"Ok, the first rule is, magic is only for the chosen. What's the next rule?"

"The next is, magic only works on non-living objects," she curled her legs and wrapped her arms around them tightly, resting her head across the little flat space formed by the tops of her knees.

"So you can't do magic on me?" he continued to feel amused.

"No, not on living things," her head popped up, and she leapt to her feet, "I'm sorry, I have to take this again." Opening her hand, her small white device lay in it once more, and she peered at it intently.

Rising slowly next to her, he felt certain it had appeared out of thin air. Keeping his eyes fixed on the glowing screen, he could see her viewing some sort of video. When she had finished, she curled her fingers and the item vanished; *oh my God.* "Where did your phone go?"

"Not now, we have to leave." She held out an extended appendage, "Take my hand, Charlie. I can't take you with me if you don't choose to go."

He stared at her slender fingers, her perfectly manicured nails slightly longer than what he preferred. Pursing his lips, he returned his gaze to hers, considering what he had gleaned so far.

"Please, Charlie, we must hurry!" she shook the digits at him, smiling slightly to encourage him.

With slow reluctance, he grasped her hand, only for a moment aware of the warmth. An instant later, they were standing outside of a building. The air felt cooler, with a dense fog or mist pressing in from all sides. Looking around, he could see the lot filled with rows of matching vehicles, only varying in the color. Recognizing it as a car dealership, "Holy shit!" he gasped, "How'd we get here?"

Remembering his shoes were still sitting on the beach, he glanced down at his should-have-been bare feet, once again covered by his canvas sneakers. His mouth gaping, he began to tremble, "What's happening to me?"

"You're fine, Charlie. Let me work for a moment, and then I will explain everything."

A woman and her son exited the building, chattering merrily. "I don't get it," the short brunette spoke to the boy, waving her ring of keys at him. "It wasn't working and we had to use the key, but now that we're here, it's fine."

"Sounds like magic," the boy teased with a giggle.

"Right," she joined in with a soft laugh, "Our guardian angel is looking out for us again."

Slipping into the vehicle, the pair rolled away, off to finish their errands and continue their day.

His brow furrowed deeply, Charlie demanded loudly, "Ok, so what was that all about?"

Shaking her head ever so slightly, Clarisse cut her eyes over at him, then ran her hand down his arm, "They are some of my clients; or charges we sometimes call them. I'm their Guardian Angel, Charlie. It's my job to look after them."

Glaring at her, he stammered, "You really expect me t' believe that?"

"No," she confessed, "Not yet. So let me explain. It really is my job to look out for certain people." Opening her left hand towards him, her phone-like device appeared. "This is my Seeker."

Blinking at the dark screen, he knew there had to be a trick to it. *Things don't just appear out of thin air.* However, that is what he saw, as best he could describe it. She brought her hand up, and it was empty; she opened her palm flat, and it was just… there. Lifting his eyes from the device to meet hers, he waited for her to go on.

"A Seeker is a communicator, if you will. I know it looks like a cell-phone to you, but it is much more than that. This is how I see what is happening with my clients, wherever they are. It is also how I get instructions from the great ones."

"The great ones," he huffed, "You mean God?"

"No, Charlie. You are outside the world of men, now. You must learn to see the bigger picture. There are two great ones in our world, two deities. They are a set of twins, a male and a female, who have been here for many thousands of years."

He nodded, still staring at the flat screen, "So they send you orders on here, and you go save people," he pulled his hands to his hips. "But they looked fine, so I don' get it."

"Of course they were fine," she smiled at his linear train of thought, aware it would take time for him to adjust. "I altered their future. Earlier today, I was messaged by Destiny that the pair needed an alteration. I sabotaged her key fob so that her car would not unlock with the remote, and they had to use the hidden key to get inside. She is a sensible young woman, and made the stop here at the dealership, to have it looked at. But there is nothing wrong with it, and the mechanic sent them on their way."

"I don' see how sending them on a wild goose chase is helping them," he frowned, sounding cross.

"Oh, Charlie," her laughter tinkled lightly, "Take my hand, love." She made the offer, and he reluctantly obliged.

THREE

Destiny and Fate

AN INSTANT LATER, the couple sat at an outdoor cafe, a selection of food before them. Only mildly surprised this time by the sudden shift in scenery, Charlie wrinkled his nose at the spread. "I'm still not hungry," he muttered. "An' you didn't explain why you made her key not work. Only, she was driving the car t' get there, so obviously it did work."

"Yes it did," Clarisse agreed, "I simply prevented the door from opening. I didn't want to strand them; only to give them a nudge." Leaning forward, she folded her hands under her chin, her elbows on the table, "You saw the fog, right?"

"Yeah, what about it?"

"In the bad weather, an accident lay in their future. But Fate had not put it there, so Destiny allowed me to change it. To alter their path, so they could avoid it." She stared patiently, waiting for him to process the concept, then continued. "What Fate has deemed cannot be avoided, Charlie."

"Destiny and Fate," he squirmed, "Those are the twins?"

"Yes, those are our guiding spirits," she confirmed.

"You said 'our,' so that means there are more of you... Guardian Angels."

"Yes," she went on, "There are quite a few of us in this world. Those who have been chosen to live on this side of the plane, to guide and protect the future of men; whatever that future might be."

He looked away for a long moment, his gaze falling on the people around them, going about their busy lives and taking no notice of the couple seated at the table. "Where are we?" he demanded, aware that they were not in Florida, best he could tell.

"New York," she offered quietly. "I like this place. I find it restful, and come here often when I'm not busy tending to my clients."

Continuing to watch the crowd, the young man sneered, "You're crazy, you know that?"

Clarisse blinked her long lashes at the young man, allowing him to work his way through what he had learned. Sensing a new message, she opened her hand to peer at her indicator. Touching the icon, she viewed one of her favorite clients, her eyes growing misty for a moment. Closing her hand, she straightened her features, "I'm not crazy. I am as real as you are, and I have a very important job to do. There are dark forces in this world, and I am the hand that sees to it they are kept at bay."

"You're sayin' there's things out to get us," he quipped, finding her story amusing.

"Yes, Dark Angels are always about, pushing destruction and ruin wherever they can."

"So that makes you, what, a Light Angel?" he laughed out loud, mocking her with his tone.

"Yes, I'm a Light Angel, Charlie. Sometimes called a Summer Angel; I draw energy from the warmth of the sunlight."

"And you use it on non-living objects to change the destiny of people," he chuckled again, his disbelief obvious. Pinching his arm, his laughter continued; *I'm gonna wake up any minute.*

Staring at him, she could tell he wasn't buying her story, and she would have to go deeper if she were to win him over. Reaching across the flat surface, she offered him her palm. Watching his eyes glare at her extension, she prodded, "Don't be afraid, Charlie."

Swallowing hard, the sandy haired male raised his brown eyes to glare at her soft blue orbs, "What if I don' wanna see any more?"

"We don't have a choice," she whispered. "Just a little more, hun, and I promise; I'll take you back to your parents."

Lifting his hand, he caught the edge of the table, giving it a squeeze. Sliding his fingers across the glass top, they trembled slightly when he reached her. The moment his flesh touched hers, the chairs were left empty in the small gathering, no one around them taking note.

FOUR

The Dark Side

CHARLIE FELT CHILLED, a dark alley surrounding him. Blinking a few times, he could make out the graffiti covered walls that lined the narrow passage. To his left stood a large dumpster, filled with smelly garbage, some of which had fallen onto the ground and polluted the air. Coughing at the foul mixture, he leaned against the wall, trying to catch his breath.

"Where the hell are we now?" he demanded, more unhappy with their journey at every stop.

"We're still in New York," she supplied in a quiet voice. "Visiting one of my oldest charges," she continued softly, "One I have tried so many times to help."

Following her gaze, he could make out a row of cardboard boxes leaning against a wall. The air was cooler in the shadow of the tall buildings, and he emitted a small shiver when he noticed the sound of rustling paper coming from inside the structure. "Is someone in there?" he gasped. He had heard of street people, but had never seen a homeless person beyond those who begged on corners back in Texas.

"Yes," she agreed softly, "He's in there."

"So, why don't you use your magic and build him a place to live?" the boy scoffed more loudly, before realizing they might be heard. Inching closer to the makeshift sanctuary, his voice took on a lower disgusted tone, "What kind of Guardian Angel are you, if you let this happen to him?"

Clarisse could hear the accusation, aware that he did not understand. "I cannot make the choices for him, Charlie. I can provide the path or the means, but in the end, it is up to the client to follow them. The woman you saw earlier; she had to choose to make the stop. That is what altered the future for them, and avoided the accident. She could have chosen to continue on, and I would have been powerless to stop it."

"So it is with this man," her extended palm indicated her subject, "Many times, I have lain obstacles in his path. Tangents that could have led him to a better place. He chose to sidestep them. The choices we make dictate the lives we lead, Charlie," her face grew drawn, and he could see the sadness pressing down upon her.

"You're saying he wants t' live like this?" he glared at her incredulously.

"Not in so many words," she whispered, "I'm only saying, he chose not to take a different path. This is where we are, and this is how it is." Her face shifted, fear taking the place of sadness, "Oh, no!"

"What?" he bit angrily, "Another client you have failed t' protect?"

"No, Charlie," she opened her palm, staring at her small white communicator, "It's time. Come away, precious," she stepped forward, and he noticed that her wardrobe had changed, and a long white gown flowed about her. Grasping his arm, she guided him away from the box, their backs to it.

Hearing a commotion behind them, the young man paused. Turning to look over his shoulder, she gripped him tighter, preventing him from doing so. He could hear the cries for help and frowned into her horror-stricken features.

"Don't look, Charlie!" she implored in a raspy voice.

"What's happening?" his eyes wide as saucers, he panted, hearing the sound of the cardboard shelter being ripped away and blows being laid upon its occupant.

"Fate will claim him," she confessed, a tear spilling over and moistening her lashes, "I am duty bound not to interfere."

The ruckus continued, striking fear into Charlie, his chest growing tight as he struggled to breathe. Staring into her clear blue orbs, her comrade felt confused, "But... you're his Guardian Angel! Stop them!"

"I can't," she cried, oblivious of the two men who had ceased their beating and began to paw through the remains, searching the body and its premises.

Holding him, inhibiting him from seeing their actions, Clarisse trembled in the darkness of the alley. Sliding his arm around her slender frame, Charlie pulled her closer to him, his own horror overwhelmed with the urge to protect her. He could feel the warmth of her air brushing his cheek, keeping the heaviness of the shadow that surrounded them at bay. A moment later, the two men ambled up the narrow path, walking right next to the couple.

"Did ya get a whiff o' this stack o' cash?" one of them wafted a fist full of bills, "Couple 'o grand here, but it smells like ass!" he cackled.

"Half o' that's mine," the second man rejoined with a punch to the arm, "An' I don' care what it smells like! It all spends th' same."

Charlie could feel his gut wrench at their degrading demeanor. "Oh my God," he breathed, turning enough to see the bloody corpse and what remained of his home strewn across the pavement. "You hid us, so they couldn' see an' attack us, too," he deduced, gripping her more firmly, "Like some kind o' cloaking magic." The very air around them seemed to grow even colder as he held her thin frame.

Glaring at him in surprise, she inhaled deeply, holding it for an instant before releasing it loudly; "Sure, Charlie," she nodded.

Turning back to face her squarely, the young man jumped at the sight of a hooded figure, standing over her shoulder.

"Well, who is this now?" the stranger spoke in a low moan, removing the cover from his head.

Instantly, the girl stiffened, emitting a small cry. Spinning in her new friend's arms, she placed herself between the two males, and shook her head slowly, her heart pounding at the surprise visitor.

Looking him up and down, Charlie noted he wore a black robe, his skin equally dark; human shaped, but definitely something else. "Who the hell are you?" he demanded, his voice filled with bravado.

"I am Gous," the new arrival hissed.

"Go away, Gous," the blonde screamed, wiping at her tears while straightening herself to her full height, "You may have taken the beggar, but this one is mine!"

Low laughter rumbled from beneath the dark cloth, "Is he now?" His beady brown eyes shifted to auburn, "What if I'm still hungry?" His dark lips parted, exposing sharp white teeth.

"Can't you fight him? I mean, what is he?" Charlie stood closely behind her, speaking quietly into the back of her head. His instincts on edge, he recognized the ebony stranger as a foe.

"I am a Dark Angel," Gous proclaimed, the sound of his voice grating on the boy's nerves like nails on a chalkboard. "I am the minion of Fate."

Shifting, her white robes billowing around her, she called back, "You have no business here! Be gone, before I summon the Keeper!"

The Dark Angel laughed at her challenge, "Are you frightened, boy?" His eyes had grown brighter, the red overpowering the brown, looking more like glowing embers. When Charlie failed to respond, he addressed his nemesis, "The beggar was always mine. I only took my time, allowing him to suffer before I devoured him. Watch yourself, Clarisse. I think you are mine as well," he ended with a sneer.

"I will never be yours!" her jaw clenched. Leaning closer to her, Charlie's arms tightened around her waist as if to hold her from physically attacking the interloper. "Away with you!"

Too frightened to speak, the young man waited. The hair on his neck standing on end, he watched a hand slide out of the robe, rising slowly to caress her trembling chin with an extended digit.

"Enjoy your time while you can, Summer Angel. The darkness is coming, and there is nothing you can do to stop it!" His words filled with ominous foreboding, he turned his back on the couple, disappearing the instant his hood had been dropped back into place.

FIVE

Powers That Be

TURNING IN CHARLIE'S ARMS, Clarisse stood nose to nose with him. His hands slid up her back, relieved that the stranger had left them, and the couple forgot their surroundings for a moment. Lifting her chin, her soft white lips tenderly brushed against his before he parted them to deepen their kiss.

Growing aware of his pull upon her, she withdrew, "No, Charlie." She exhaled loudly, caught up in the moment with him.

Staring at her features, so close that they blurred, he asked for the second time, "What's happening t' me?"

Glancing at the beggar who was no more, she released her companion, catching his fingers, "I need to refresh." An instant later, they sat upon the beach, with the hot sand beneath them.

Looking up, she allowed the warm sun to cascade across her face, while the young man cast his gaze hurriedly around them. *It looks like the same place,* he contemplated, noting his bare feet. On the left, his shoes lay next to him. Frowning, he wondered if they had ever left the spot at all. *What if she did all of that through some mental illusion?* "We've been here all along, haven't we?" his words sounded terse, his accusation clear.

"No, Charlie," she spoke softly, aware of his internal struggle. "I brought us back to Miami to warm up and recharge." She lifted her hand, opening the palm to indicate the large ball of fire above them. "I haven't done anything to you. I can only use my powers on non-living things; what you feel is real. What you see is true."

"Why did those men attack your other client?" he asked quietly, "Why did you hide me from them, but not him?" His voice quavered, feeling as if he were a pawn in some game the girl played with the Dark Angel.

Her brow furrowed, she had no choice; he would have to be told the truth about the powers that be. "Gous sent the men to do his bidding. He can make men act, but he cannot do things to them directly, any more than I can. It is part of the protection that mankind was given when the planes were formed. He wanted to claim the beggar's soul, but he cannot simply kill men outright."

She glanced over at him, nervous about what she would divulge. "That is the source of his power, love; the essence of the living. That is why I can never influence a living thing. To do so taints us. It destroys any who partake of such dark magic, weakening the being forever, and transforming them into a loathsome and vile creature."

Charlie stared at her, his mind racing. After a long pause, he squinted at her, "Are you saying that thing was once a Light Angel? And that he went dark because of what he did?"

Her eyes shifting to take in the waves before them, she admitted, "I guess that would be one way of looking at it. Although, I am not certain that he was ever what you would call light. Most men are not, and the power of the dark minions is growing. Mankind has forgotten the ways of caring and love, and embraces the evil in the world more and more."

Her golden locks fell in a shiny curtain, blocking her face from view. Daring to catch the strands, he pulled them back so that he could see her profile, "How long have you been an angel?" he asked quietly. "Were you once a living person, like me?"

Her lip quivered when she turned to take him in. "I was a living person. I was caught in a rift. An instant when another's fate was imposed upon my own." She swallowed visibly, then confessed, "I'm not really from Maine. I grew up in London, with my parents. When I was seventeen, they decided to move to America, and I went with them. We were on board the Titanic," her voice dropped. "I'm sure you know what happened to it."

His eyes wide, he could feel his lungs refusing to work. Forcing a deep inhalation, he stammered, "You're sayin' you died over a hundred years ago?"

She shrugged, "Yes, although that was not my fate. I had been placed in one of the lifeboats. But a drunken woman, flailing about in panic, knocked me out into the freezing ocean, and I drowned. My body was lost to the sea, and I had no choice, but to become a Light Angel." She pursed her lips, then popped them open with a small snapping sound, "About a dozen angels were taken from the aftermath, and the rest were devoured by Fate and his minions."

Charlie felt sick, his chilled flesh crawling, even beneath the warmth of the sun. "That's horrible," he managed. "And you've been watchin' over your charges ever since?"

"Yes," she smiled, "Not that I mind it. I rather enjoy it, almost as if it were a game."

"And how long have you been... watchin' me?" he eyed her, wondering if she would lie.

"Since you were born, Charlie," she smiled shyly. "I have often wondered these last few years if Destiny had chosen you for me; to be my mate." Her blue eyes shown, unsure how he would react to the idea.

"Your mate!" he exclaimed. "I have to go home! I have my parents, and college, and a whole lot o' other stuff I need t' do. I can't get all caught up in some dead girl; in some... ghost!"

"I am not a ghost, Charlie!" she snapped, angry at the insinuation, "It was just a thought! Besides, it will be Destiny who does the choosing, so don't worry."

"But that's why you've taken me on this crazy journey, today, isn't it? Why we met and what you've been planning, showing me all of this?" his voice too high and loud for comfort, he berated her callously.

"No, love," she shook her head, wiggling her toes into the sand, "I know better than to try and manipulate people. That is the path that leads into the darkness." Her eyes cut over to him, "I was only hoping, that is all."

"Then in that case, I'm ready to go home now," he stated flatly. "I think I've heard enough about you an' your crazy alternate universe. Besides, my parents are probably wonderin' where in the hell I am, an' it's about time I stopped makin' them worry."

"Your parents aren't worried... or looking for you," she soothed. Shaking her head, the girl stood, waiting for him to join her. Deep down, she had wanted their adventure to last for several days, and that would give him time to warm to the idea of being with her. But the untimely arrival of Gous had spoiled that plan, and the young man had discovered too much, too quickly.

"You must prepare yourself, Charlie," she spoke softly. Casting her gaze upon his handsome features, she took his hand with her left and wrapped it with the right. "I have told you much, but I have not shared it all. What you will learn next will be the hardest for you."

SIX

Caught in a Rift

ALLOWING HER TO HOLD HIM, Charlie pushed his feet into his shoes, and cast the sand from his shorts with his free hand. "Whatever," he quipped, grabbing her roughly when he was ready.

An instant later, they stood in a hospital, in one of the corridors. Looking around wildly, he gasped, "Now what the hell are you up to?" He could see a row of patient rooms around the outer wall to his right, with a large nurse's station in the center of the square, to his left.

Spinning around, a woman that had been standing at the counter next to them passed unchallenged through both of their bodies; first hers, and then his. His mouth agape, he glared after the short blonde. "I knew you weren't really taking me places! This is all in my head!" he screamed loudly. "See? They don't even notice us! They can't hear us or anything!"

Grasping his arm, she squeezed him firmly, "Calm down, love. I told you, this part will be the hardest." She wiped his bangs to the side, clearing his vision with her long pale fingers. "You're right, they can't see us; or hear us for that matter. But, we are really here. We're in a different plane. Remember me telling you that? We are outside the world of the living."

His eyes darting around, his chest heaved, and he only half listened to her. After several minutes, he moved to the side; the women passing through him more than he could bear. Watching them come and go for a while longer, he puckered his lips. "So why are we here?" he blurted, half suspecting the reason. *I'm dead. I'm fucking dead.*

Sliding her warm fingers into his, she guided him down the hall. Entering a small room, a young man lay in the large bed, a myriad of hoses and tubes attached. From the doorway, he could see his mother slumped in a chair, and his father standing at the window. Moving closer to the pair, he could see the man's eyes were glazed; he stared, unseeing, into the afternoon sun.

"What happened to me?" his voice fell across the silence. Waving his hand in front of his father, he knew before he did that it was a useless act.

"He can't see you, baby," she comforted, "They can't hear us, either."

"I know," he agreed, shoving his hands in his pockets, "We're in another plane." Turning slowly, he faced the machines, aggravated by their beeping and humming; the only sound in the small space. Stepping towards the bed, he lay his hand on the railing, feeling the cold metal in his grasp. "Well?"

"You were hit by a car. Rifted by another's fate. It had just happened, when we met this morning, and Destiny summoned me to your side."

"Rifted; like you," he nodded slightly.

"Yes, like me."

Tears came without warning, and he asked in a squeaky voice, "Can I please be alone?"

"Sure, Charlie," she nodded gently, turning to the door and exiting through the wide-open frame.

The young man wasn't sure what to do, staring at himself as if he were another person. Watching his chest rise and fall, lying on the mattress before him, he could hear the hiss and pop of the machine. After a long while, he shifted to study his parents. *Man, they look so old,* he observed.

His mind turned, and he thought about the lives the three of them had led. He had grown distant from his parents the last few years; pushing them away. He suddenly longed to reach out to them, to pull them close and tell them everything would be ok. *But I can't,* he lamented. At that moment, a man in a long white coat entered the room and closed the door.

"Mr. and Mrs. Phillips," he cleared his throat, "I have the results of our tests."

His father turned from the window in slow motion, while his mother sat in the chair; if she could hear, she gave no sign.

"Your son's brain functions have ceased. The machines are all that are keeping his body alive. I realize this will be a very difficult decision for you, and you can take all the time you need." He reached for the door, pausing with his hand resting on the handle, "I've been a physician more than a decade, and this part never gets any easier. I am truly sorry for your loss." Pulling the knob, he allowed the portal to close behind him.

As if on cue, his mother began to wail; a low loud shriek that would have woken the dead, if it were possible. In an instant, Charlie closed his eyes, picturing Clarisse; wishing nothing more than to be by her side and away from the pain and unraveling that would take place in the tiny space.

Finding her, he materialized next to her slender form, standing on a stretch of concrete sidewalk, overlooking the sea. Taking her hand, he gave her a squeeze. "So what do I do now?" he asked softly. "Am I their Guardian Angel?" he smiled slightly, "Or is that still your job?"

"Oh, Charlie!" she sobbed, flinging herself into his arms. "I'm so sorry. I don't want you to think I wanted this. I never wanted this!"

"I know," he exhaled loudly, wrapping her tightly. "I just don't know what will become of them, with me gone. They don't really love each other; not any more. They haven't in years. Without me to bind them together… who knows what will happen to them."

She whimpered quietly, her forehead pressed against his. "There's something else, love. One more thing you must know."

The setting sun to his right, and the ocean to his left, he traced the line of her back with a firm grasp. Her hair shimmered in the fading light, and he smiled, "Well, don't leave me hangin'! Am I gonna be a Dark Angel?"

"No, Charlie, you won't be a Dark Angel, unless you choose to be," she grinned. "In fact, you could choose to be dark… or light. Or, you could choose to go home." Her crystal blue eyes flittered to his soft brown orbs, drinking him in.

"What do you mean, I can go home?" He stiffened, catching the hand she had been using to rub his shoulder. "You said I was dead. That I was hit by a car! The doctor even told them, and I even moved like you do! Through thin air, with only a thought."

"I know, and for right now, you are very much a part of my world," she worked her way closer to him, pressing against his warmth, "But, you were rifted. That means, Destiny will intervene on your behalf, if you ask her to."

"I don't understand," he hesitated, "If that's true, why didn't she intervene for you?"

"Because my body was gone, Charlie. You can't live in the physical world without a body. I'm just a spirit now," a tear trickled down her cheek to drip unchecked from her jaw. "You were right. I am a ghost. Trapped for a hundred years in servitude. There is nothing for me to do, except continue to serve the living. Or be mated to Gous."

"Gous?!?" Charlie shoved her away, "You were serious about that? I thought he was jus' messing with you!"

"No, hun," she sniffed loudly. "He's been following me for a while; stalking my clients, taking them here and there. He wants me; so far I have kept him at bay, but I don't know for how much longer."

Frowning, he squeezed her hand, "This is all so confusing. Let me get this straight. I can choose to stay here, with you, as a Light Angel. Or I can turn Dark, and use people to do my bidding, feeding off o' their souls. Or I can go home to my parents, an' have my life back, jus' the way it was."

"Sure, love. That's more or less accurate. Only your life won't be exactly what it was. You were still injured. You will still have to heal, and there may be things about your body that won't be like they were. But yes, you could go back," she hesitated. "But if you do, you won't remember me. Nor will you remember the second plane, or any of the things you have learned today."

His air catching in his throat, he coughed slightly. "How long do I have to decide?"

"Until they cut off the machines keeping your body alive. When that happens, you will have to choose, either to return and give your body life, or to let it pass, and stay here with me."

"Ok," he agreed quietly, sliding his fingers along her jaw, trailing the line beneath her ear and into her hair. Leaning forward, he pressed his lips to hers, a soft kiss, tasting her before parting them to delve into her warm mouth more fully. Ending the affectionate display a moment later, he implored, "Give me time to decide, ok?"

"Sure, Charlie!" she grinned from ear to ear, hoping he would choose the path that would make her the happiest in the end.

SEVEN

By My Side

THE SUN DIPPED below the horizon, and Charlie felt an odd ache in his chest. "It's time t' go home, I guess," he smiled slightly, trying to remain positive, "Where might that be?"

"Wherever we want it to be," she replied with a hint of mystery. "I'd like to show you a bit more, if you're willing."

Nodding, he placed his hand in hers, content to allow her to guide him. In an instant, they traveled from the east coast to the west, the light blindingly bright after adjusting to the dark.

"Whoah!" he shielded his orbs, noticing the deja vu before him, "We just watched this, didn' we?"

"Of course," she giggled, adjusting his fingers in her grasp. "But I love sunsets; and sunrises."

"Yeah, I think you have a thing for oceans, too," he smiled, flicking his gaze up and down her thin frame.

"Of course," her voice grew wistful, "It is a part of me." Cutting her eyes over at him, she wondered if he understood. Either way, it was time to continue her lessons. Opening her hand, she peered into her Seeker, noting which clients were turning in for the night.

"Soon, we will travel to the other side of the world," she explained, showing him the tiny display. "I have a few clients in Australia, and a few more in Europe."

"So while these guys are asleep, you're off tending t' them. Don't you ever sleep?"

"No," she twisted slightly, the warm evening breeze fading with the sun. Blinking a few times, she traded her clothing for a light sweater and white denim, looking up and down his tall frame. "You can change too, if you like. Close your eyes and envision what you would like to be wearing."

Doing as she commanded, he leaned his head back, allowing his brown orbs to close, then open slowly while still looking at the fading blue above them. "Gosh it's beautiful here," he lowered the lids again. When he opened them, he found he wore a long-sleeved tee and a pair of jeans with sneakers. "Was I the one controlling the shoes before?" he recalled finding them in the sand and on his feet with no explanation as to why.

"Yes, you were," she turned him so they could walk along the pier. "You've been learning to control it the entire time we've been together. A little practice, and it will be like second nature."

"Ok, well, tell me this. First off, why do we bother wearing clothes, when no one else can see us. And second off, if this isn't my body, why do I feel cold?" he could hear the questions forming in rapid succession inside his mind, and wondered how much she would actually divulge.

"We wear them because of custom, I guess. I don't really know. We can assume whatever shape and appearance we want, but mostly, I look like myself." She shifted her eyes over at him, finding his observations strange.

"Do you always train the new Summer Angels?"

She laughed out loud at that one, "No. I have never trained anyone. None of my clients has ever become an Angel before."

"Never?" he gasped. "In a hundred years, you would have thought at least a few of them would have made it to heaven."

"This isn't heaven, Charlie. Not like what you are thinking. I can't say that it doesn't exist, and that some of the souls make it there, but that is not where we are. Many souls are devoured by the Dark Angels."

"Yeah, about that," he grimaced, "You said that you absorb your energy from the sunlight, which I get. But Gous feeds off of death. I don't see how there's enough for there t' be too many of them, if that's the case."

"Oh, that's not all that he is able to use. Not exactly. He feeds off of souls, but one does not have to die for him to absorb part of it," she guided him over to a bench, taking a seat. "He feeds off of the negative energy that is produced when men do things to hurt one another."

"Wow," he shook his bangs out of his eyes, "So those two guys beating up that beggar. That gave him more than the soul alone."

"Yes," she agreed, "It tore parts and chunks away from the two men, and he devoured that as well. Lying, stealing, injuring, all of those things feed the dark side. All he has to do is give the humans a push; their natural instincts take over, and the deed is done."

"Ok, so why don't you just push them the other way? Use your magic to make them do good things for other people instead of bad?"

"I told you why; we cannot use our power on the living."

"Because it doesn't work," he deduced.

"No," she sighed, "Because it makes us dark. A Light Angel who uses power over the living will become dark. There is no way to avoid it."

"So you use your power on inanimate objects. How does that make the humans be protected?"

"Well, it's like an art, really. You have to learn how to blend every-thing to make it run smoothly. If a human can sense that you have altered something, they get agitated; you don't want that kind of disruption. You want them to be calm, and act as if you are not even there," she patted his leg.

"Because technically we aren't really there," he stared at the ground before him, the weight of the issue a heavy burden at the moment. "So when do I get my own Seeker and clients and all that stuff."

"When your body has grown cold, you will be welcomed by Destiny. She will present you with a Seeker, and a short list of clients, which will grow over time."

"A short list?" he turned up a palm in surprise, "How is that gonna protect everyone, if we only have a small number? There's like seven or eight billion people on this planet."

"Right," she agreed, "But they don't all get Guardian Angels. Only those chosen by Destiny. The rest are left to Fate, and he does not care what happens to them. They are like cattle or sheep, only here for the feeding and entertainment of his minions."

"Fine," he swiped his hand, as if he were wiping the discussion away, "What about the Keeper? You told Gous you would call him, so what does he do?"

Clarisse smiled, watching the last of the sun sink into the water in the distance. "You don't miss a thing, do you? Keeper is Destiny and Fate's father. He maintains the balance between the two halves; the darkness and the light. Gous may think that they are growing strong, and eventually will win, but I don't think that will ever happen. Keeper ensures that there will be balance. In fact, I think he is a little partial to the light."

His brow furrowed, "If he's partial to the light, does that mean he can destroy the Dark Angels?"

"Yes, I guess you could say that. He collects them, and absorbs them into himself. Recycles them, if you will. They are his source of energy, although he doesn't actually need to feed. His power is perpetual, as if it comes from every corner of the world," she outlined the connection for him.

Leaning forward, Charlie placed his elbows on his knees, laying his chin on his hands, "Well, that's no good." He sighed loudly, "If he can destroy them, and rid the world of them forever, why doesn't he?"

"There cannot be light without darkness, Charlie," her voice grew quiet. "And no darkness without light. Come," she stood abruptly, "Let us be off to visit more of my clients. I can't wait to make the next stop with you by my side."

He grinned at her, finding her observation amusing. "I still have things I wanna know," he insisted.

"Yes, but you will not learn them all in one day," she offered him her hand.

Allowing her to take them to their destination, he slid his fingers into hers, while for a brief instant his mind drifted to his parents. Then they were gone, and he was again focused on the girl, her mission, and his new life, if he could call it that.

EIGHT

A Gentle Push

ARRIVING at their target location a moment later, Charlie once again squinted into the morning sun. "Where are we now?"

"Germany," she smiled brightly, "One of my clients has a new baby, and I want you to see it."

Standing to the side of the path next to her, he could tell they were in some type of park. A short distance away, a couple ambled along, side by side, pushing a large carriage. As they passed, Clarisse grasped his arm, guiding him along next to them so they could observe the infant.

"Aww," he moaned, "It's sleeping."

"Yes, she's precious. It took many months and a good deal of help for them to conceive," she admitted with pride.

"I thought you weren't allowed to use magic on people," he glared at her.

"Oh, I didn't," she grinned sheepishly. "I helped with timing, that's all." Opening her Seeker, she offered it to him again, "See this line?"

Charlie stared at the screen and what appeared to be a graph, "Yeah, what does it mean?"

"This is her life-line," she indicated the woman before them. "See the two grey areas along the edges?"

"Yup, I get those, too," he nodded.

"You want the life-line to stay between the grey zones. If it crosses into one or the other, something is out of whack," she touched the screen. "When that happens, you have to make an adjustment, depending on your warning code."

Watching the flicker, he understood. "So you make changes to her environment."

"Yes, changes that act as a gentle push, to alter her course."

"Unless she's like the beggar," he recalled his former lesson, and the sad result.

"Yes, sometimes, they refuse to take a different path," her mood grew somber. "But they must have free will, Charlie. You must never force them; that is the path to darkness, and it will destroy you."

"I get it," he placed his hand beneath hers, turning the device so he could see it better. "What does this red flashing mean?"

Seeing the mark at the same time, she gasped, "It means we have trouble. Gous is attacking one of my charges!" Offering her hand, they were off in no time, arriving outside a small house bathed in darkness.

"Where are we?"

"Ohio," she breathed, "Try to be quiet, in case he or other Dark Angels are about."

"Oh," he held back, unsure of what to do. Following her flowing locks, he moved around the outside of the house, watching and listening. Hearing a crash on the opposite side, they dashed around the corner in time to see a pair of legs disappear into the broken frame.

"Quickly!" she grasped his fingers, whisking them to the second floor, where her clients were sound asleep in their bed.

"We must wake them!" she whispered loudly.

Shrugging, Charlie reached over and gave a large vase a shove, causing it to crash to the floor. The man sat straight up, and Charlie quickly deduced that he was naked. Looking over at the woman, he could see the outline of her in the dim light, realizing that she was as well. Grabbing the blanket, he started to yank it off of her, when Clarisse hissed, "Not obvious!"

He stared at her for a moment, before grasping her meaning. "The guy's down stairs!" Snapping his fingers, he disappeared, leaving Clarisse in a mild state of panic.

An instant later, she was next to him, observing as he began to shove everything off of the kitchen counters, allowing it to fall onto the hard tile floor with a loud crash. The burglar had been climbing the stairs when he heard the noise below, followed a moment later by the sound of footsteps above. Realizing the owner had awakened, and his attack no longer a surprise, he retreated by way of the back door.

Running through the kitchen, he observed the broken items with a frown, unsure what had caused the issue. However, realizing he had no time to investigate, he opened the rear exit, and sprinted across the yard, making it over the back fence only seconds before the porch light lit up the entire area.

"Man, that was close!" Charlie huffed, grinning at his fair-haired companion. "And you're right, that was kinda fun."

"No, it wasn't fun!" she countered angrily, "If we hadn't come right away, and had some fast thinking on your part, my clients could have been killed!"

He felt torn by the tears on her cheeks, watching the mistress of the property assess the damage in her bathrobe. "I'm sorry," he stammered, "I guess you care a great deal about the people in your charge."

"They are all I have, love! A few hundred people, and they are like my family." Her face had grown flushed, the anger boiling inside her.

"You should calm down," he cautioned. "Being upset won't help you make good choices."

Turning her back, she shoved her face into her hands, sobbing quietly. Stepping towards her, Charlie ran his hand across her shoulder, working it beneath her silky strands. Locating her spine, he ran his digits up and down, giving her a firm caress. "Don't worry, Clarisse. They're fine."

Deciding the couple would be ok, and that his companion needed sunshine and rest, Charlie slid his hand around, taking her hand in his. Clasping her fingers, he squeezed, and waited for her to return the gesture, indicating she was ready to travel. A moment later, they were back in Germany, standing on the path where he felt certain the couple and the child would comfort her.

Feeling the warm rays on her flaxen hair, Clarisse raised her face to drink in the golden energy. Turning and opening her eyes, she smiled at him for a moment, "Thank you!" but the look quickly shifted to horror.

Spinning on his heel to follow her gaze, he could see the carriage laying on its side a few hundred feet away, the man and woman who had been pushing it nowhere in sight.

NINE

Fate's Minion

THE COUPLE RAN down the path, a low squeal of agony trailing behind the girl's long flowing locks. Reaching the cart, she grabbed the side, dropping to her knees and feeling inside; no blankets and no baby. Resting back on her haunches, she pressed her face into her palms, her shoulders jerking as she bellowed.

Laying his hand on her crown for a moment, Charlie studied the carriage, then moved around for a closer inspection of the underside. "The axle is broken," he commented loudly.

"Of course it is," a deep round voice added from behind them.

Standing rapidly, the girl faced the old man, "Father!" Flinging her arms around the plump figure, his white hair and beard were even more so than her own.

Charlie noted the wrinkled face that implied his age, and the white robe that he wore, similar to that Clarisse often chose to don. "Father, huh," he stepped forward, offering him a hand.

"Hello, Charlie," the gentleman shook the appendage firmly. Turning to the girl, he reached up, as she held at least four inches on him in height, to brush away her tears. "There there, Summer Angel, your clients are safe."

"Are they?" she screamed, relief flooding her features, "How? Why? What happened?"

"I gave them a little nudge," he indicated the wounded contraption with an open palm. "I noticed a Dark Angel lurking about while I visited one of my own charges. I decided it was wise that they return home in short order. The man will come for the device later, from what I understand."

"Oh my, thank you so much!" she gushed, throwing her arms around him once more. Allowing herself to shed a few more tears of joy, she clung to him for a moment before stepping away, prepared to give her new friend a proper introduction.

"Father, this is my friend, Charlie."

"Yes, I know who Charlie is," the old man smiled, his eyes twinkling, and for a moment the boy thought he looked an awful lot like Santa Claus.

"Pleased to meet you, sir," he gave the man a small bow, "You were on the Titanic as well, I presume."

With a bewildered look, the man in question shook his head, before making the connection, "Oh," he laughed heartily, "No, I was not. Father is my name, son. I had another," he ran his pudgy fingers around his wide round belly, "But that was many centuries ago, and it has long since been lost. I'm not even sure if I can recall what it was!" His hand lifted to caress a few strands of the girl's hair, "I am the oldest of the Light Angels, and therefore have been given that moniker out of respect."

Smiling, Charlie liked the man instantly, "So, why did you send them home? Is it unusual to have Dark Angels about? I thought they were everywhere, from what I have seen so far."

"Unusual, no," he replied, stepping closer to the boy and dropping his voice, "But strange things are afoot in our realm. Your arrival here among them," he grasped Charlie's arm, "You have met Gous, yes?"

"Yes," he paused, nodding, "He took one of Clarisse's oldest clients; a beggar in an alley."

"Gous has had his eye on our maiden here for some time. He is a conniving sort, and I fear that the stability of our leadership may be at risk."

Frowning, the girl grasped the old man's arm as well, "Let us depart from this place, Father. I feel a chill, and this is not a conversation for dark ears." Offering the pair her hands, each grasped a milky white palm and she transported them to an open air cafe, placing them in seats with warm air moving around them as the sun shone down brightly. "This is better, don't you think?"

"Better for a moment," the newcomer smiled, "But it won't keep for long."

Her face downturned, her features drawn, she nodded. "I am aware of Fate's minion, Father. And I am aware of his desire to possess me. Yet I resist." She lifted her gaze, "Charlie was rifted. I do not see a connection between his arrival and the shadows that hang over our world. Destiny will return him to the land of the living, if that is his desire; I am certain of it."

"Be careful, Clarisse," he waggled a finger at her, "Destiny may honor his request, but I do not believe his arrival was purely an accident. You see, this boy is special. Look how quickly he has taken to our ways; accepted our laws and governing. Weeks and months should a new angel practice to perfect his craft; and yet only hours old, he is flitting about and trying his wings."

Charlie stared with his mouth slightly agape, "You think I was brought here on purpose?"

"Of course," he smiled, "What I am not sure of, is who is behind it. I think that perhaps Fate has grown tired of sharing this planet with Destiny. It could be that Gous is his hand to affect that change. Or even likely, Gous wishes to replace the twins, with Clarisse at his side."

The girl audibly gasped, "How dare you, Father! How to speak such blasphemy!"

"Peace, my child," he wafted a hand at her, "I merely suggest what I have seen. And two angels united can be a powerful force; if one were light, and one were dark, imagine the power that they would wield. It could be enough to topple the ancient ways, and where would that leave mankind?"

"But Keeper would never allow it!" she slapped the table lightly with an open palm.

"Do not place too much faith in Keeper," the old man warned, "He is much older and wiser than any of us. If he has deemed the end of men to be at hand, it is not for us to say or argue his demise."

"Wow," Charlie spoke up, "This old codger speaks in more riddles than you do!" He laughed, trying to make light of his insult, but his obvious displeasure with the exchange remained uncloaked.

"Don't be rude, Charlie," the girl spoke quietly. "Father is only intending to help, I am certain." Turning her attention to the old man, she lay her hand over his, "Please, Father; continue."

"There is nothing else to say, my child. Only that you must choose your path carefully. Remember the rules, and hold to your beliefs." Turning to glare at the young man seated across from him, he squinted slightly, as if he were trying to see him more clearly, "I think you will have a greater part in the end of this than you realize at this time."

Leaping to his feet, he continued, "But I must be off. I have my own clients to tend to." Leaning over, he kissed the girl lightly upon her forehead, and disappeared.

"Wow," Charlie breathed again, "What did you make of all that?"

"I don't know. I'm just glad my clients and their child are safe," she lamented quietly. Opening her palm to glare at her Seeker, she flipped through the screens, watching what was happening in the lives of her charges. "Here, let us go and check in on a few of these. I see an adjustment or two that can be made; I could do it from here, but I would like to show you the results."

Laying her hand across the table, she waited for him to grasp her firmly. When he had done so, the transport took no time, and they were standing in a very old group of structures, on a narrow road; a small suburb on the outskirts of London.

TEN

An Angel's Work
———————————

"THIS'S A NICE PLACE," Charlie observed, having a look around.

"Yes, it is," Clarisse agreed. "One of my oldest clients has lived here for many years. The last few, a cancer has been growing inside him, and very soon it will be discovered, if he does not die today."

His brown eyes grew wide at her casual mention of the man's passing, "Are you serious?"

"Oh, yes; quite!" she grinned, "Relax, love. He fell several hours ago, and is lying in the woods there behind his house," she indicated the stand of trees that ran behind the dwellings. "One of his neighbors is outside now, and I can affect my alteration that will lead to his discovery, before his demise."

Leading him into the edge of the woods, she watched the neighbor's dog patiently. When he had moved close enough, she produced what appeared to be a small rabbit, that danced and teased the beast. Once the canine had taken up a pursuit, the white fur raced ahead of it, down the path with the owner trailing along behind. "See how easy that was?" her straight white teeth gleamed.

"I didn't know you could create animals," he gasped, "And how did the dog see it? If we are invisible?"

"Animals are different," she explained. "Men live in the physical world; we in the magical plane. Objects, such as the dog, are caught in between, a bridge connecting the two. The man could not see my magic, but he followed the dog that had run away. In a few minutes, he will discover my charge lying on the ground, and call for an ambulance. I'm afraid it will be a long ordeal to retrieve him, but in the end things will work out in his favor."

"But if you knew he was going to break his leg in there, why didn't you change that part instead?" he stared at her in confusion.

"Because," she exhaled slowly, keeping her tone in check, "When they go to set his bones, they will discover his cancer. If he had not broken his leg today, that information might have remained hidden until it had become untreatable. And of course, if I had not sent the neighbor into the woods, he would have perished overnight, and his body remained there for several days."

"And you can tell all that from your Seeker."

"Yes; I told you, it is a very powerful device, and the more time we have before, the better the plan we can lay. I only wished it could always be so," she smiled at his understanding.

"Do Dark Angels have Seekers?"

She glared at him for a long moment. "No, not that I am aware of. They are a gift from Destiny, and I am sure if an angel were to turn, she would strip it away from them."

"I see," he ran his fingers around his mouth, observing the dog's owner hurriedly exiting the treeline, and jogging towards his home. "An' now the call will be made, an' a new timeline will be in effect for your client."

"Yes," she beamed, "All is well."

"Have you ever let anyone die?"

Her features instantly morphed, as if he had slapped her, "Certainly not! I would never intentionally allow harm to come to one of my charges! I swear to Destiny, Charlie, sometimes you astound me!"

He chuckled lightly, moving around the small area, examining the taller trees before shuffling out into the open yard. Spreading his arms, he allowed the light to beat down upon his upturned face, "You know, I used to do this when I was a kid. I love the feel of sun on my skin. It seemed… tingly; refreshing somehow."

"Father did say you were special," she recalled aloud. Opening her device, she smiled faintly, "Time for another miracle, hun." Holding out her hand, she waited for him so that they could zip away to the next location.

Arriving a moment later, he could see a tall building being constructed. Shading her eyes, the girl obviously searched for someone among the throng of men moving around the site. Glaring up at a tall tower, she pointed, "There he is!"

At the top of the scaffolding, Charlie could see a man in a hardhat, moving around, not unlike any of the others who were a part of the crew. "Ok, what does he need?"

"Well," she opened her hand, "From what I see here, he is going to have an accident in a few minutes; one that will injure several of these men. Of course, the incident itself is hazy, and I'm not sure exactly what's going to take place. This often happens when large numbers of people are involved; things get muddled and we have to pick our way through."

"If he were gonna have an accident, why didn' you push him to take the day off this morning?"

"Because, I could not see that far ahead this morning, hun. I told you, the further we can see, the better we can plan, but sometimes, we have little or no warning. Like your accident…" her voice trailed away. "If only I had known."

Watching the tower sway slightly in the wind, Charlie could feel a knot in the pit of his stomach, "We need to hurry," he whispered hoarsely. In an instant, he left her on the ground, and stood next to the man in question, who turned unexpectedly and passed through him. *That's gonna take some getting used to,* he chuckled to himself. Noticing a few power lines strewn about the deck, the man's boots became tangled with them while he milled about, and he began kicking them out of the way.

With a flick of his wrist, the young man brought the cable to life, as if it were a snake, and wound it around the man's ankle, his heart fluttering at the violent rocking motion of the tower. Looping the other end, the tool still attached, he anchored it to the support pole of the building an instant before the deck dropped from beneath them.

Charlie could hear the scream of the girl the loudest over the calls of the men surrounding the scene of the crash. The scaffolding lay in a mangled mound of metal and wood, and the rest of the crew wasted no time reaching the rubble to uncover those who were buried. "Hey," he spoke softly, giving her shoulder a squeeze from behind her.

"Oh, Charlie!" she exclaimed, throwing her arms around him, "I thought you had fallen!"

"Well, no," he corrected, "And it wouldn't have hurt me, if I had, would it? Or am I still bound by the laws o' gravity?" he grinned at her, somehow pleased at her concern.

Smacking him playfully on the arm, she swung her gaze to locate her client, who dangled from the building. Bound by a bright orange electrical cord that acted as a rope, it tethered him to the skeleton frame. Flailing his arms and calling to the men below him, she could tell he was all right, even before she opened her device, "You did it, love," she breathed. "You saved him."

Lifting her gaze to stare into his chocolate brown eyes, she queried, "How did you know that's what was going to happen?"

"I dunno," he shrugged with his right shoulder, showing her his palm while the left held her in a half embrace, "It seemed logical, I guess."

"Maybe so," she agreed, an inkling of fear tickling her gut. The couple remained long enough to see the man cut down and safely on the ground before joining hands to return to Miami.

ELEVEN

Duty Calls

FINDING himself seated on the beach in Florida, Charlie curled his toes into the sand, noting the coolness of it in the early morning light. "I like this place," he commented quietly.

"Yes," she agreed softly, "It is a favorite of mine." Dragging her fingers through the clumps of granules, she sighed loudly, "So, how do you like my world, love?"

"It's ok, I guess," he leaned back on stiff arms, watching the sun creep higher, almost clear of the water's edge on the horizon. "I think I would get used to it."

"You don't sound like you've made up your mind yet."

"I haven't," he admitted in a timid voice. "I think I need to visit my parents again before I decide."

The girl shifted, a cool breeze blowing long strands of her hair out behind her. Her delicate features remained calm, keeping her internal struggle hidden. She knew she must leave the choice to him, but she felt an immense ache at the idea of his returning to the world of the living.

"I understand," she eventually admitted in a hushed tone. Opening her palm, she stared at her device, making a few adjustments and relaxing into the warmth of the rising sun. Not noting anything that required personal attention, she closed her hand, giving him a small smile. "Let's go and see them, then; shall we?"

Getting to their feet, he stumbled slightly, catching himself against her, pulling her into an embrace. "Do they have… love… in this plane? I mean, like; real love?"

"I suppose that we do," a warm flush covered her cheeks. "I'm fairly certain that I love my charges, very much in fact. Why do you ask?"

"I dunno," he shrugged with a single shoulder, "I think this world would be very lonely. I mean, right now, it's not so bad, because you're showing me around, an' we're together. But after things are finalized, an' I'm welcomed by Destiny, I doubt that it will be this way. I think you an' I might hardly see each other. I'm not sure that I would like that as much."

She grinned, squinting slightly, "I agree; having you with me has changed my perspective as well. I will miss you when you go, hun; whichever path you choose." Ending the conversation by offering her hand, she whisked him away to the hospital, where they discovered his parents standing together in his tiny room.

Entering the small space, Charlie smiled, noticing that his father leaned against his mother in a half embrace, each of them holding a cup of coffee. They were talking quietly to one another, while observing their only child, who lay connected to the tubes and hoses. Nodding once, he turned to the girl. "Ok," he smiled, "I'm ready."

"You don't want to stay any longer?"

"Nope; I jus' wanted to see what was happening. It looks like they're still working things out." He glanced over at the couple. "I haven't seen them so much as touch each other in years; this's a good sign."

Assuming that to mean he would be ready to leave them, she smiled, grasping his hand and taking him to the patio cafe in New York. While they sat, she explained a bit more to him about the Seeker. In the midst of their discussion, a chill settled over her. Craning her neck, she cast a wary glance around them.

"You felt it too, didn' you," he whispered much quieter than the two of them had been talking.

"The cold?" she replied softly, "Yes, I felt it."

"Is he close by?"

"I don't know. Maybe we should leave."

"And where are we going?" a familiar voice hissed.

Turning in his chair, Charlie discovered the shorter man standing behind them, grinning down from above. Rising slowly, the young man held his gaze, "Gous," he growled, "What're you doing here?"

"Whatever I please, actually," he clasp a hand full of blond hair, allowing it to pour through his fingers. "I thought you would have run home to momma by now."

"No, actually I was thinking of staying," he countered.

"Really," he bared his pointy teeth, "You are a very strange Light Angel. I guess you want to fight me then, over the girl perhaps."

Clarisse had gotten to her feet as well, and Charlie moved, positioning himself between them. "If I have to," he stated flatly.

His laughter even louder, Gous leaned slightly towards him, "I guess she hasn't told you what would happen if you were to lose."

Gripping his arm, the girl did her best to convey her warning without forming the words. Folding his arm, Charlie caressed her digits, the touch curling his lips slightly.

"I'm not afraid of you, Gous," he stated flatly, "But now is not the time for confrontations. Clarisse and I have work to do; duty calls."

"Does it," his dark eyes gave no sign of what he might be thinking, "Then by all means," he wafted a hand at the people seated around them, oblivious to their presence. Taken with an urge to demonstrate his power, he commanded, "Choose one."

"What?" his opponent stammered.

"Choose one of them; to be a demonstration. She has been showing you around, wooing you to her, if you will. It is my turn; choose the one that will be the example."

Charlie's eyes darted about the crowded eatery, about thirty hungry diners enjoying their late breakfast. "I'm not going to choose anyone," he clipped. "You have no reason to harm any of them."

"Oh, but I do," the Dark Angel grinned even wider, waving a single extended digit side to side. "It's my job, you see; duty calls." With that, his eyes took on an auburn color and began to glow as if they were bright embers. A moment later, one of the men seated at the table next to them began to call out.

"Hey," the patron demanded loudly, "Where's the damned waiter?"

Hearing his boisterous exclamation, the young server made an appearance, only to be berated as soon as he did.

"Where the hell have you been?" the man stood, his hands forming fists.

"Hey, Tom; sit down," his companion cut in, "Leave the kid alone, would ya?"

Tom passed an angry glare between the two of them, then took a swing at the seated gentleman, knocking him clean out of the chair. Not waiting for his friend to get to his feet, he squatted over him, landing several blows to the prone body. Other patrons began leaping to their feet, their tables being jostled and overturned in the ruckus. A general chaos ensued, with several more patrons joining in the brawl.

As if in slow motion, Charlie watched the fight grow, seeming to suck in those around it like a vacuum. Turning to look at the shorter man next to him, he could see his eyes had begun to glow bright red, and he could tell the Dark Angel was gleaning essence from at least some of the diners, if not all of them.

Thinking quickly, he surveyed their surroundings, looking for a way to bring the mayhem to a halt. *Nothing obvious,* he reminded himself. Noting the hose coiled beneath the shrubs along the edge of the building, he mentally punctured the rubber, causing shoots of water to spray out over part of the crowd; only a small amount, the effect appeared minimal.

Seeing the leak, the waiter grabbed the apparatus, and opened it up full blast, bringing the disruption to an abrupt end. Tom rolled over, looking about at the soaked and angry faces glowering down at him.

"What happened?" the source of the chaos queried. Getting to his feet, he hoisted his friend up, wiping at the blood dripping from his cheek and chin, "What the hell is going on, Doug?"

"I have no idea," the other man slapped him on the shoulder, laughing slightly, "But the next time you get pissed at the waiter, I'm leaving."

Grabbing his arm, Clarisse guided Charlie away, "That was fast thinking," she praised, her gaze swooping around in search of their nemesis, "Gous disappeared as soon as he realized you had won."

"What the hell is wrong with him?"

"What do you mean? He's a Dark Angel. He lives for chaos and ruin."

"Oh," Charlie grunted, "That's it. So what does he think, that he's gonna recruit me?"

"Maybe," she shrugged, grinning back at the group of people working to straighten up the mess. "It bothers me though, that he has taken an interest in you. I think we need another word with Father. I think he knows more than he let on."

"Hmm, you could be right. How do we find him?"

"Let me give this a try," she replied softly, opening her device and scrolling through the options.

TWELVE

Guardian

IT ONLY TOOK a moment for the girl to locate her old friend. Holding her hand out, Charlie clasped it eagerly, and the pair traversed the large distance, landing on the other side of the continent. Spying the older man while he watched his charge, the couple waited until he was free to converse before making their presence known.

"Ah, Clarisse, and Charlie, still with us I see," the old man called out to them in a friendly manner.

"Yes, Father," the younger man greeted him amicably, "But we've had more trouble from Gous."

"Well, I'm not surprised," he moaned, "I told you things are coming to a head."

"So what do we do about it, exactly?" the young woman queried.

"You could request an audience with Destiny; let her know what you have discovered."

"But we have not really discovered anything, yet. We were hoping you could give us more," she smiled at him sweetly.

"I'm afraid I have given you all that I can," the old man shifted his weight from one foot to the other. "I don't really know anything else. And I do have work to do. Go see Destiny if you want; or wait and see what else develops." Giving the pair a small wave, the man disappeared before they could protest any further.

"Hmp; that was no help at all," Charlie lamented, kicking at a clump of grass.

"Yes, he left in a hurry," she agreed.

The cold chill fell over them only an instant before both were knocked to the ground. Rolling over quickly, Charlie struggled to get to his feet, angry to see the dark flowing robe hovering above her white gown as she sprawled on the dirt.

"Clarisse!" he called sharply, oblivious to the danger in his eagerness to defend her. Stepping forward, he clamped his hand down on the shoulder of his enemy, pulling him away from her. "Leave her alone, you bastard!"

"Oh, angry are we?" Gous taunted him, noting the girl appeared to be unconscious. "I do not want to destroy her, Summer Angel. Do not force my hand."

"Then get away from her," Charlie demanded loudly. Sidestepping, he worked his way around so that he could see her slow movements, aware that she may have been tapped from the cafe and the flight, and in no condition for a confrontation. "I told you before, I'm not afraid."

"Well, you are a fool. You should give up this nonsense and join our cause," he raised his hand, indicating he had not come alone. Out of the shadows, two other dark forms emerged. "You have something we want, little man, and we are not leaving without it."

Charlie's eyes darted over to the girl, longing to reach down and help her to her feet. However, he feared the movement would prompt an attack, and he needed to remain focused in order to defend himself. "Oh yeah," he played for time, "What is it then?"

"A special kind of magic," the sharp teeth tossed back, "We want it. We want you on our side."

"You're going to challenge the twins, aren't you," he shook his brown locks, inching closer to the girl, who had made it to her knees.

"Whatever gave you that idea," Gous sneered. His eyes flickered brightly an instant before the wave of energy crashed into him, and the young man found himself reeling. Managing to stay on his feet, he returned the blast, only causing the Dark Angel to laugh.

"Charlie, no!" Clarisse warned, getting her legs beneath her and preparing to fight him as well. Holding up her hand, she indicated her intention, and the other two joined in, sending dirt and rocks flying at the pair.

"Hey! That actually hurts!" Charlie bellowed, not having realized that they could use the physical world against them in that manner.

"Of course it does," she frowned, "We are in a different plane than the living organisms, but the non-living matter can pass between. Like the cold, Charlie."

He grinned brightly at the epiphany, "Holy shit! Why didn't you tell me that before?"

She only glared at him, aware that they were in deep trouble, "This is no time for questions and answers, lo- "

Gous cut her off with a large stone flung into her gut, knocking the wind out of her. Sinking to her knees, the tears trickled down her flushed cheeks. Emitting a low wail, her hands began to tremble with rage, "Destiny, please!"

Watching the scene unfold, Charlie became overcome with rage, using his own body to shield her from the next wave of debris, and helping her stand, "We have to do something!"

"Like what?" she continued to struggle to hold her feet, "We are outnumbered, and overpowered," her legs buckled once more beneath her. "I'm so sorry, baby."

His hand dropping to touch her crown, he splayed his fingers across her cotton locks. "It's ok. We won't go down without a fight." Spinning, he ripped the fence from the ground behind them, hurling the pickets at the trio across from him.

Clarisse watched as his eyes began to glow, a deep auburn, followed by a soft red, "Oh, no, Charlie!" The wind caught her cry and carried it away.

Continuing his angry torrent, the young man traded blows with the trio, the sky over them darkening, and a bolt of lightning struck a pole nearby. A loud crack and boom echoed between the dwellings, knocking them all onto their backs. Rolling quickly onto his feet, Charlie continued his assault, his eyes burning like flames when he began tearing away portions of the wood and shingles from the nearest house, hurling them at their enemy, while shielding himself from their attacks.

A moment later, he noticed that the group had been joined by a very tall man, with bronze colored hair and skin. Unsure of who it might be, he could only guess that this was Keeper. *He traps them and devours them,* he recalled. The thought occurred to him that he no longer qualified as a Light Angel, and would more than likely be one of the destroyed.

Turning his attention to the girl, he could see the tears glistening on her cheeks. The wind whirling around him, he grinned, "I don't care!" His chest heaved, his vision clear, "As long as they don't get you, then I have served my purpose!"

He shouted as loudly as he could to be heard over the storm, "You are my charge! I'm your Guardian Angel, Clarisse!" He held a hand out towards her, his heart pounding wildly inside his chest, "I love you..." his voice trailed away as he spun, throwing himself headlong into Gous, taking him to the ground, and rolling with him, bringing limbs from the tree above crashing down upon them. A moment later, he could hear nothing but silence.

THIRTEEN

A Place for All

CLARISSE PULLED herself to her feet, stumbling across the uneven ground and dropping onto her knees next to the boy. Tears dripped from her quivering chin, her fingers searching for his face and clearing away as much of the dirt and leaves as she could. "Please, Keeper. Please don't take him!"

The bronze figure moved closer, silently inspecting the havoc the group had created. His angry glare cast over the bodies of Gous and his companions, and with a wave of his hand they were removed. Returning his glowing gaze to the young man who had fought to protect the Summer Angel, and perhaps even their realm, his voice rumbled, "There is a place for all, Clarisse. You know he does not belong here."

She continued to weep for several minutes, holding her dearest friend's hand. "I know this, Keeper. But it is his right to choose, is it not?"

"Then take him to his parents, and he will choose." Reaching down, he laid a firm hand on the boy's chest. "Arise, my son," he called to him. "The bravest of the Guardian Angels; take up your future, and hold your head with pride."

Coughing loudly, Charlie rolled onto his side, dimly aware of his soaked clothing, and the two figures that flanked him. "What the hell happened?" he groaned.

"You saved me!" Clarisse called to him eagerly, "You saved me," she repeated more quietly, cutting her eyes over at Keeper. "Thank you. I am forever in your debt." Lifting her head, she noted the tall dark haired woman observing them. Her long white gown flowing in the gentle breeze, she waited over Keeper's shoulder. "Destiny!" the girl breathed, "I mean, your highness!"

"Please," the greatest of Light Angels held up her hand, "Destiny will suffice. But we must go. The time has come for our newest Summer Angel to make his choice, and so we must return him to his body that he may do so." With a wave of her hand, the three of them materialized inside the hospital room once more.

Standing in awe, Charlie looked around at the cramped space, noting that Keeper had joined them as well, and stood in the corner to observe the proceedings. "What do I do?" he asked in a meek voice. "I don't really understand."

"It is your time, Charles Phillips," Destiny spoke with a firm voice.

"My time," he repeated, placing his hand over his heart.

"Yes. Your time to choose. You have sacrificed much for our cause, and I will repay your bravery tenfold. You may remain with Clarisse, and she will be your mate, if you so choose," she wafted her hand, indicating the young woman who instantly broke into a wide grin of agreement.

"But," the matriarch continued, "It is not your time, and you have been rifted from your home, and the life that was meant to be yours. If you so choose, I will return you to your body, while it still lives, and you may continue, until Fate claims you."

Charlie stared at her, blinking slowly, waiting for more. When nothing else came, he cast his eyes around the group. Noting that Keeper wore a stoic expression, he realized that he would get nothing from the elder. Turning his gaze to his parents, he could see them leaning against one another while standing over his bed.

His father's left arm held his mother tightly, the hand comforting her by stroking her arm firmly. "Beth," he spoke softly.

"Yes?" the woman replied.

"It's time to let him go."

Charlie could feel the flush wash over him, fear that they could see or hear the gathering.

"They do not sense our presence," Destiny informed him, in an effort to relax him. "Choose, my child."

"It'd take a real miracle, wouldn' it, John," Bethany whispered. "It'd be a great miracle indeed if we were to get him back."

Turning to pull his wife against him, John shook in small spasms as he wept; "It would be, love. That it would be."

Inhaling a sharp breath, Charlie turned his gaze to Clarisse, who stood watching him with doleful eyes. Swallowing hard, he flicked his tongue over his lips, the words he needed to speak the most difficult of his life. "I got a lot o' things left on that side to finish," he began quietly.

"I know you do, love," she replied softly, extending her hand towards him. "And it's ok." She smiled, aware of her promise to allow him to choose. "I want you to be happy, Charlie." Warmth spread through her being when their fingers met and entwined as they had been the first time she had touched him.

"I'm not going to remember you, am I," he flicked his free hand at his body lying beneath the sheets. "If I go back, that's what you said. I'll forget all about this place, and everything that happened."

"That's right. But it's ok. I'll remember," she smiled more brightly, squeezing him, "I'll remember for both of us." She bit her quivering lip, "And you can go and do all of those things… for both of us."

His father moved, reaching over and hitting a switch; the one the doctor had indicated would stop the machines when they were ready. Listening to the silence, Charlie nodded, "Goodbye, Clarisse."

"Goodbye, Charlie," she smiled, and in an instant, he was gone.

FOURTEEN

Only a Miracle

CHARLIE COUGHED HEAVILY, his eyes fluttering a few times, then squinting into the glare. His arms felt heavy, and an elephant sat on his chest for a moment. Struggling to breathe, he closed his deep brown orbs, aware of the shrieks and screams of his parents. Lying still, his thoughts jumbled and turned while he fought the confusion that muddled his brain.

A few minutes later, he stared at the ceiling through narrow slits. With a grimace, he tried to speak, "What the hell's goin' on?" His voice came out hoarse; croaking in an odd manner. Raising his hands, he felt the residue of the tape on his cheeks, and the tenderness of the cuts and bruises that covered his face, "What happened to me?" he tried again.

He could feel hands pressed against his skin, and another rummaging through his hair. Cutting his eyes over to the left, his mother's face lay right next to his. "Mom?"

"Yes, baby," she squealed, clinging to him as best she could in his prone position. "You were hit by a car, son," she nuzzled him, breaking into loud wails of joy.

Running his hand over her back, John tried to comfort her, "Bethany, calm down; you're scarin' the boy!" He grinned from ear to ear as he spoke, in shock over the turn of events. "Only a miracle, could have saved you son! Only a miracle…"

Four days later, the trio sat in the Miami airport, waiting for their flight to Texas. Perched on the edge of her chair, Beth Phillips continued to dote on her only child, as she had been since he had awakened from the dead.

"Are you sure you don't need anything?" she quipped, reaching over to adjust his clothing over his bandaged chest.

"I'm fine, mom," he sighed loudly, "Really. Go wait with dad, please!" He grinned, watching her join her husband, sliding her arms around her mate for a tight embrace.

Charlie smiled at the couple; *I guess being dead really changed a lot of things in my life.* He would never complain though; seeing his parents in love was a beautiful thing.

While he watched, a girl sank into the chair next to him, adjusting her oversized bag onto the space between her slender rear and the arm rest. "Oh my God," she complained under her breath.

Glancing over at the tall blonde, Charlie's mouth grew slightly twisted, "Hi."

"Hey," she countered, her eyes darting up and down at his collection of bumps, bruises, and bandages. "Wow; looks like you took quite a beating," she commented offhandedly.

"Yeah, I, uh," he rolled his tongue around inside his cheek for a moment, "Had a fight with a car. I'm pretty sure I lost."

"You've got about as much luck as I do," her brow furrowed, and she flipped her long golden locks behind her. "We were on a cruise; the ship sank."

Her matter-of-fact tone took him by surprise, "You're joking!"

"Not at all," she pursed her lips, "Over four hundred people drowned. It's a real miracle we survived." She chuckled softly, "Guess both our guardian angels were working over time this summer!"

"Yeah, Summer Angels," he agreed, showing off his set of pearly whites.

She shook her head, smiling a little more broadly, "I never heard them called that before," she cut her crystal blue eyes over at him. "What does it mean?"

"I dunno," he shrugged, "I guess I heard it somewhere. Anyways, I'm Charlie," he offered her his hand.

Taking the appendage, she held it gently, noticing the deep marks where his IV had been. Tracing the area lightly with an extended finger, she whispered, "Wow, you weren't kidding."

"Nope," his Adam's apple moved up and down as he swallowed, "They told my parents I was dead. Then, when the machines were cut off, I woke up."

"An' you don' remember anything?" her eyes grew wide.

"Not a thing. Well, I remember the flight out of San Antonio, and a little bit about the day we arrived in Miami. That's about it," he nodded at her again. "You look really familiar, though. Maybe in a straw hat."

"Oh my God!" she exclaimed loudly, "You're that kid from the airport! We were standing outside together before the flight; you have the whiney-ass mother!" Her face flushed instantly, "Shit, I didn't mean to say that; I'm so sorry."

"No, it's ok. Back then, I would tend to agree. Today, not so much. My parents have changed a lot in the last week," he wafted a hand towards the couple that stood by the glass, stealing kisses on occasion.

"Wow, that's so cute!" she agreed. "You live in San Antonio?"

"Austin," he grinned, "As soon as the semester starts."

"Shut the front door! Me, too," her laughter tinkled lightly. "I'm Donna, by the way. And I'm very pleased to meet you." Noticing the attendant calling everyone to line up, she grimaced, "I guess it's time to go, Charlie. Maybe we'll meet again later; get to know each other."

Watching her walk up the ramp a few minutes later, he smiled to himself, knowing they would in fact be getting to know each other better if he had anything to say about it.

PART II
Dark Angel

Prologue

"KEEPER!" Gous screamed into the darkness, a black so deep no light could penetrate it. "Let me out of here!"

"He can't hear you," a stranger's voice answered his call.

"He can hear," a second replied to the first, "But he doesn't care."

"Why don't you two shut up," Gous grumbled, "Keeper! I know you are listening!" Leaning against a wall, he moved about the cramped space, discovering his cell to be a two by two box, with only room to squat if he chose. "I guess it's a good thing I'm not BIG AND FAT!" he bellowed.

"Ugh, pipe down," a reprimand came out of the abyss.

"Why don't you come in here and make me," the Dark Angel laughed his challenge, a low rumble that swelled and filled the surrounding chambers. "It's not fair, Keeper! You know what Destiny has done! She has broken your laws! She openly defies *your will!* How dare she allow Clarisse to return to the plane of the living. How DARE SHE defile another's body!"

"That's impossible," the stranger's voice answered for Keeper. "You should shut it before you are devoured."

"It's not; I saw! He knows what she has done," he laughed again, his voice lower while he spoke to his prison mate, "But she won't get away with it."

Screaming again, he addressed the greatest of all angels, the one that is neither light nor dark. *The angel who maintains the balance.* "KEEPER! When you are ready to dispense justice, be sure you let me know..."

FIFTEEN

Things Change

"LET'S GO, CHARLIE!" Donna called to her boyfriend for the second time. "My grandmother's party is in an hour!"

"I know, I know," he dashed down the stairs of their new loft apartment, "I don't know what you're in such a hurry for; that old woman is crazy," he teased.

"Charlie!" she glared at him with mock anger, "She's not crazy! She has dementia, and there's a huge difference."

"Yeah, yeah," he grinned at her, "You know I'm teasing," he gave her a quick peck on the cheek. Taking her hand, they exited the front door and scurried down the street. With practiced hands, he put her into the passenger seat of their tiny hybrid.

Watching the traffic, he waited for the break and dashed around to climb behind the wheel. Easing out of the parking space, he grinned in relief, "It's getting easier."

"Of course," she agreed, also referring to the traffic patterns on their new block. Flipping the visor down, she added gloss to her pretty pink lips. Closing the tube, she sighed loudly.

"You think she'll remember you this time?" Charlie tapped the wheel, anxious for her.

"I don't know," the lanky blonde watched the trees passing overhead, admiring the new leaves. "I think she's been getting worse. I hope it doesn't happen to me when I'm her age."

"Yeah, me either," he chuckled, using his blinker to get out on the highway. "See, we're gonna make it, right on time." Laying his hand over on the console, he waited for her to take it, then gave her a squeeze. "I love you, Donna."

"I love you, too, Charlie," she replied softly, resting her head against the seatback behind her.

Arriving at the nursing home a short time later, the couple exited their compact car and set the alarm. Reclaiming her warm fingers, Charles Phillips led his girlfriend, Donna Parker, up the concrete steps. Taking a left in the main hallway, he pushed the button to the elevator.

"Thank you for doing this," she interrupted his thoughts. "I know there are better things you could be doing on a Saturday afternoon."

"Ah, baby," his expression flickered surprise, "This's important to you. An' that makes it important to me, so there's nothing I'd rather be doing. No need to thank me," he smiled. Leaning towards her, they shared a brief kiss before the shiny metal doors parted and they made their way down the hall.

The entrance to Grandma Parker's room propped open, the couple easily glided inside, skirting the small gathering and taking up a spot along the left-hand wall of the seating area. "I see you!" the girl's mother called, bringing them up short.

"Hi, mom," Donna turned to the woman, forcing a smile. "Sorry we're late," her eyes subconsciously darted to her companion.

"Don't apologize to me," the older woman quibbled, pointing at the guest of honor, "You need to go and see her."

"She doesn't know me," the blonde flicked her long tresses, releasing him to work her way through the onlookers, "Hello, Grandma Parker."

Seated in a wheelchair, the elderly woman looked up into the soft blue eyes of her granddaughter, unable to make the connection to her name. "Hello," she mimicked the girl, her fingers shaking as she reached for her hand. Clasping it firmly, she pulled on her arm, so the girl knelt beside her. "How are you, child?"

Donna smiled politely, aware that her use of the term meant she, in fact, had failed to recognize her… again. "I'm good, Grandma." Staying with her a few minutes, she waited for something to distract her, and then slipped away. Locating Charlie, she sidled up to him, her eyes wide with frustration.

"That good, huh?" he teased.

"Yes," she pursed her lips, blinking back tears.

Madeline, Donna's mother, watched the young couple from the other side of the room. Inhaling deeply, she steadied herself, playing hostess to the party and keeping up appearances to the best of her ability. An hour later, the guests began to say their goodbyes, departing to get back to their busy lives.

When Donna and Charlie approached her, she clasped her daughter's hand, giving it a small shake. "I need you to stay, sweetheart. We have something we need to discuss."

Forcing her pink stained lips into a smile, she agreed reluctantly, "Sure mom. We can stay a few more minutes."

Watching the room clear, Charlie studied the older woman nervously, considering the last time she had needed to talk. *I hope she's not about to give Donna a hard time again.* The first incident had been seven months ago, back when they had first started officially dating at Halloween. Taking a sip from his cup of punch, he allowed his thoughts to drift back to their first meeting, and the dark cloud that had seemed to hang over them ever since.

"Charlie, this is my mother, Madeline. Mom, Charlie," she had made the introduction nervously.

"Hello, Charlie," the ebony haired woman gave the boy a cursory grin, her gaze darting back to her daughter. "Something else that's changed, I guess?" she did not hide her displeasure.

Her expression one of horror, the girl stammered, "What's wrong with that? Things change, mom!"

"Yes, I know. Since the accident this last summer, everything about you has changed…"

Charlie replayed the memory often, as it had struck a chord with him on two levels. First, he had also been in an accident this past summer; one that had changed his life completely. *Every day is a miracle,* he reminded himself, watching the last of the party guests exit the small room. *She and I both had a brush with death;* a fact that had connected them somehow, and gave their relationship strength.

Of course, where all the changes in his life had seemed to be for the good, Donna's friends and family had not accepted her emerging personality so willingly. When her mother approached, he could tell it was going to be another discussion about how she wasn't the girl she used to be.

Deciding to skip the lecture, he made the first move, giving the woman a small nod, "I think I'll wait outside." Not pausing to hear her reply, he exited, closing the door behind him.

Looking up and down the corridor, the tall young man studied a painting that decorated one of the walls. Hearing their voices raised on the other side, he couldn't understand the words, but the meaning rang clear. When the girl opened the portal to join him, he grabbed her arm and escorted her to the lift, exhaling a loud gush of air, "That's why you should pass on stuff like this," he hissed. "She just uses every time she sees you to complain."

"Oh, Charlie," the girl sighed, leaning against the wall of the moving compartment, "I wish it were that simple."

"Donna, you realize the accident was nearly a year ago?" his blood boiled.

"I know, Charlie!" her voice grew tense, "But she's right. I'm not the person I was before that fateful night..." her voice trailed away at the confession, knowing he only saw half of her dilemma.

"Of course you're not," he defended her, "You survived when the odds were against you. So what if everything about you has changed! You're entitled to be who you wanna be," he sighed loudly, tugging at his brown waves, "No, who you need to be!"

Cutting her gaze over to take him in, she inhaled deeply and pushed the air out noisily through her nose. Giving him a small smile, she whispered loudly, "Thanks, Charlie. You're the only person who understands."

The doors opened at that moment, back on the ground floor and she reached for his hand, ready to return to their car, their home, and the life they had been building together for the better part of a year.

Inside the vehicle, he grimaced at the sinking sun. Rolling down the windows, he commented offhandedly, "Let's enjoy the air." Taking care, he backed out of the space and worked his way into the traffic before asking, "You wanna stop for dinner?"

"Sure," she smiled, her long blond wisps blowing lightly in the breeze, "I'd really like that. And you're right. I'm going to stop seeing my mother. It hurts too much, the way she makes me feel about... everything."

Her words like a slap in the face, his mouth hung open as he glanced at her, "I wasn't really serious about that, Donna." Guilt pressing in on him, he continued, "I don't want you t' give up on your family because of something I said."

"I'm not," she assured him. "It's because of something she said; today in fact."

Pulling into the parking lot of a mediocre spot, he wafted a hand at the sign, "Feel like Johnny's tonight?"

"Sure," she agreed with a small nod, "At least they take your order at the table; that means it's technically not fast food."

"Right," he grinned, leading her inside. Sliding into a booth, he didn't bother with a menu. The couple ate there often, and he knew what he was going to have. After he had given their petite waitress their order, he reached for the blonde's hand, "Ok. What did she say this time?"

Watching her fingers as they toyed with his, her face remained expressionless. After the pause grew long, he gave her a tug, opening the other palm to the ceiling, as if to demand a response. Shaking her head, she sighed, "I don't want to talk about it, Charlie. What she said was mean, and shows no respect for the way that I feel."

"Could you at least give me a hint?" he pulled his fingers away, allowing their meal to be placed before them, "I mean, it's hard to take your side when I don' know the details."

"Is it?" she scowled. "I thought you would always take my side, no matter what." Her eyes darted nervously, observing the diners around them. "You don't know who I was before, love. Everyone else does."

"So? I've changed too, but you don't see my family and friends complaining."

"You've become more caring. More responsible," she nibbled at her pasta dish, "Since my cruise ship sank, they say I've become reckless."

"She's still mad you dumped *what's his face* and started dating me," he laughed loudly between bites. "Come on give, what did she say?"

"She said... I've been possessed. That some evil spirit follows me now," her blue eyes glared at him intently, waiting for his reaction.

Practically spitting his last bite, he chortled, "She doesn't actually believe in that crap, does she? Ghosts and spirits? And the exorcist!" he chuckled at her mother's expense. "Come on, that's so lame."

Laying her flatware next to her plate, her features grew tightly drawn, "Sure, hun. All that's a load of crap, right?"

"You bet it is," he continued to grin, "So if she wants to push you away over something as stupid as that, let her. You can't let her drag you down, love. Life's too short for that."

"Yeah," she agreed quietly, "Life's certainly too short for that."

SIXTEEN

See the Signs

"WHERE THE HELL ARE MY KEYS!" Charlie's voice rang through the apartment, awakening Donna with a jolt.

Sliding out from the sheets, she pulled her robe over her slender frame, joining him in the living room a few minutes later. "These keys?" she lifted the ring off the end table with a tinkle of metal.

"Oh my God, yes! I swear those weren't there a minute ago," he grinned, his relief evident. "Thanks, babe!" he kissed her quickly, darting for the exit, "I'm late. I'll see you tonight, love!"

Watching the door close behind him, she rolled her tongue around for a moment, dropping her gaze to the spot where they had lain. "Weren't there, huh," she spoke aloud to the empty room. Adjusting her cover to make it more comfortable, her eyes scanned the boxes that remained. *So much work left,* she observed, clasping a few stray blond strands to smooth them. Emitting a clicking noise with her puckered lips, she checked the door latch and glided up the stairs.

Returning to the lower floor after her shower, Donna tried to push the uneasy feeling that had settled over her aside. Selecting a new carton, she used a cutter and opened the top, revealing more of her personal items; *things from a life I can't remember.* Pawing through the selection, she removed a few of them, and closed the flaps by overlapping them.

Lifting the lightened parcel, she stacked it with the others, which would be placed in their storage when Charlie had the time to do it. Taking another, she repeated the process, managing to combine a few and reduce their number significantly. When all had been dealt with, she surveyed her progress, heaving a deep sigh; *this is supposed to be wonderful. This is what I've always wanted. So why does it feel so wrong?*

Deciding to take a break, the girl darted up the stairs, pulling her phone out of her pocket as she went. Locating the number to her best friend, a small smile curled her lips, "Lunch. Definitely, lunch." Making a call, she arranged the date, her hair bouncing behind her when she came back down and set out on her way to the Metro-bus.

Arriving at the open air cafe a short time later, the young woman chose a seat on the edge so that the midday sun shone down upon her; *perfect.* Taking a menu to look over while she waited for Leanne, she leaned back in her chair. A breeze moved through, catching her golden waves and rustling them lightly, giving her a slight chill.

Sitting up straight in the seat, she laid the folded paper aside. Her eyes darting around her, she could see nothing out of the ordinary, except for the seeming drop in the temperature; *you're imagining things.* Glaring up at the orange ball of fire, she gave a slight jump when someone plopped down beside her.

"Whoop! Look who's here!" Leanne announced, her teeth brightly decorating her features.

"Hey, girlfriend," the lanky blonde replied, leaning over to give her a half hug, "Long time no see!"

"I know, right?" she continued to grin, shaking her bright red waves, "You don't have class today?"

"This afternoon, from two to four," she supplied, tossing the waiter a small wave. "I just needed to get out."

"You're all settled in then?"

"Pretty much," she admitted in a hushed tone. "But I'm not here to talk about me. How are things with you?"

"Oh, same old, same old," the girl lit a cigarette and exhaled a puff of smoke.

"Oh my God," Donna exclaimed, "I thought you quit that shit!"

"I did," Leanne giggled, "But I got a new boyfriend, and he smokes, so I picked it back up."

"Wrong boyfriend," she laughed, "I can't believe that, after how hard you worked to give it up."

The other girl shrugged, her displeasure at the mild rebuke evident, "Well, I guess we all get to choose, right?" aware that her friend seemed to be less fun than she used to be; before the accident.

An eerie feeling crept up Donna's spine, her blue eyes again darting over the crowd, "I guess so. Let's eat." Placing their orders, the girls laughed often, and shared the current events from their lives over soup and salad. When time came to be on her way, she stood, giving the other girl a tight embrace. "Take care of yourself, lady," she smiled, still not fully pleased with what she had discovered.

"You, too," the other girl called over her shoulder, curling her fingers in a wave, with her stilettos clicking as she walked away.

Arriving at their townhome after her class, Donna let herself in and made her way to the kitchen to make dinner for them. She knew Charlie had to work after school, so it would be another hour before he would be home. *Enough time to surprise him with something special,* she grinned at her plan she hoped would lift her own spirits as much as it did his.

Placing a saucepan of water on the burner, she kicked the fire on underneath. Rummaging through the lower cabinet for vegetables, a loud thump landed on the ceiling above her, sending her pounding heart into her throat. Cutting her eyes up at the fan above her, she could see the metal chain shaking side to side, "Oh God, I didn't imagine it," she whispered.

Wiping her hands on her jeans, her eyes remained clasped on the fixture as she stood slowly from her crouched position. Inching her way across the checkered linoleum, her hand trembled when she reached for a knife, sliding it out of the wooden block and gripping the handle firmly. Tearing her gaze away, she shuffled through the small dining area to the stairs.

Her left hand resting on the railing, she adjusted her fingers a few times with a single foot raised on the first step. Listening to the silence above her, the only sound she recognized was the swoosh of blood in her ears; *breathe.* Clasping the knife handle in her right hand, she began her ascent, aware that it would be useless if what awaited her was what she feared most.

Arriving on the landing, she stared into the shadow of the bathroom, able to make out the toilet and the tub inside. Raising her blade in front of her, she pivoted slowly to the right, noting the bright glow of the room. "Sunset," she surmised aloud. As if in slow motion, her trembling legs carried her forward, past the closet, through the open portal, and into the room that the young lovers shared.

Her eyes roving over the golden glow, she could see the bed to her left. She had made it that morning, and it remained pristine. Her dressing table against the far wall remained neat and organized; even Charlie's chest of drawers directly before her appeared undisturbed. Moving with greater confidence, she strutted around the bed, to the far side, tearing back the curtain and peering down at the courtyard below; *what the hell?*

Standing up straighter, Donna exhaled a loud sigh of relief. Turning on her heel, she retraced her steps, ready to return to her chores in the kitchen. Still carrying the large knife, she bounced down the stairs, purposely pushing the mystery out of her mind.

Two hours later, Charlie came in much later than she had expected, their dinner having waited for his arrival. "Where the hell have you been?" she demanded loudly as soon as he shut the front door.

Turning to stare at her with his mouth hanging open wide, he stammered, "I'm late! What can I say?"

"You can damn well give me a call when you're going to be late!" she challenged. "I had dinner ready over an hour ago, and I've been worried sick!"

A small grin curled his lips, "Oh, you worry about me, huh?" he moved closer, sliding his arms around her waist. "I'm sorry, baby, I wasn't able to call. My phone went dead," he produced the device to present it to her, "I guess it's time for a new battery."

"A new battery," she repeated absently, taking it from him and holding the button on the side, "It was plugged in all night." Watching as the screen came to life, she frowned, her anger renewed, "What the hell are you talking about? This fucker is fully charged!" she held it out to him so he could observe the bars.

"Wow!" he stepped back, shocked by her angry tirade, "I swear, it was dead!" Clamping his mouth shut, he scowled, "An' it's not like I've never been late before, so what the hell's the matter with you?"

The girl only stared at him, her body beginning to shake. Turning slowly, she muttered, "Nothing. Let's eat; I'm starved." Placing her pots and pans on the table, next to the settings she had laid out so carefully, her features remained drawn in a deep frown. The patio door to her left, pitch black, she stared out through the French panes of glass, emitting a violent shudder.

"Seriously, what's the matter," he pushed the subject, his hand finding her shoulder. "You think I'm not where I should be? You think I'm cheating on you, is that it?" He glared at her, the long strands of blond hair a curtain between them. "Answer me, Goddammit!" he grabbed her wrist, swinging her around to face him squarely.

"I can't, Charlie!" she stammered, tears spilling over and pouring down her face. "I've done something terrible, and I think it's time to pay the price!"

His turn to make demands, he grasped her forearms, squeezing her a little more roughly than he intended, "And what's that supposed to mean?"

"It means, my mother is right, Charlie. I'm not who I used to be. I thought I could hide, and that our lives would be perfect. But I can see the signs. The darkness is coming, and I'm not sure we can stop it this time." Pulling her arms free, she glanced at the meal growing cold before them. "Eat your dinner, love. I'm not hungry anymore," she called over her shoulder as she headed for the stairs.

SEVENTEEN

Call Me Crazy

CHARLIE STARED down at their plates, guilt washing over him; *damn*. He could tell she had put a great deal of effort into the meal, and he had blown it. "So much for overtime," he muttered, turning to follow her to their bedroom. "Honey, I'm sorry," he called more loudly.

Stepping into the room, he noted her hunched frame at the foot of the bed. Her face in her hands, her shoulders shook, signaling her silent sobs. Taking a knee before her, he sat back on his haunches while his fingers gently wound around her warm flesh, pulling on her arms to uncover her delicate beauty, "Hey."

Allowing him to expose her tears, her face looked distorted, causing him to inhale sharply. "Don't look at me, Charlie," she implored.

"Why?" he breathed the question. "Seriously, baby. What's happening to you?"

Flicking her moist tongue over her lips, she whined, "You'll call me crazy if I tell you. Just like you did Grandma Parker."

"No, I won't," he pushed himself up onto his knees, his arms sliding around her waist, "Baby, I love you so much. We're survivors, remember?" he alluded to their private joke. "There's nothing you can't tell me, an' I promise; I would never call you crazy."

She stared into his deep brown eyes, feeling as if they would swallow her whole at any moment. "My name isn't Donna," she stated flatly, "My name is Clarisse."

Charlie's lungs clamped down tight within his chest, as if she had knocked the wind out of him with a single punch. "Clarisse," he coughed, squinting as he tried to make the connection. Finally, unable to do so, he stroked her long straight locks, "Honey, I'm not following."

"That's why she doesn't know me," she pulled herself up straight, "Because… I'm not me. And Grandma Parker can see it somehow."

"I see," he sank back down, heels to rear, "And how long has this feeling that you're someone else been going on?"

"I told you!" she screamed, leaping to her feet, "Now you think I'm batshit psycho!" she whirled around, moving to the window to peer outside, searching the darkness for some unseen enemy.

Watching her, he pushed himself up, standing slowly, "I never said that. I don't understand. That's all."

"Of course not, you're still you," she quipped.

Grinding his teeth, he studied her, trying to decide what to do. Finally, he opened a palm towards her, while directing her down the hall, "Why don't you go have a bath, love. A nice hot soak to relax you."

The girl glared at him, "What are you going to do?"

"I'm going to go warm my dinner. After you've had time to calm down, and I'm not eating myself from the inside out, we can talk."

Staring at the bed between them for a moment, she reluctantly agreed, "Ok. Then maybe I can explain better; after I've figured out how to say it."

"Sure," he grinned, "Take your time."

Taking her nightgown, Donna closed herself into the tiny room, putting in the plug and squirting in extra of the bubble bath cream. Running the water as hot as she could stand, she slid into the lavender scented foam and leaned against the wall behind her. Closing her eyes, she tried not to think about the visions that had haunted her as of late; reminders of the first time she had met the young man who shared her life. *Back when I was a Summer Angel.*

Downstairs, Charlie stood staring at the untouched meal. Grabbing the pans, he carried them into the kitchen, shoving the items into the garbage disposal and running it hurriedly. Dropping the empty pots into the sink, he spun around, placing his rear end against the counter. His hand covering his mouth, he hoped to prevent himself from speaking; or crying out.

A moment later, he trotted into the living room, snatching his phone off of the table where she had dropped it. Glancing at the balcony above him, he could tell the bathroom door remained closed; *not good enough.* Twisting the handle to the French door, he moved into the cool spring air of their patio, closing the exit behind him.

Locating the number, he stood up straighter, shoving his free hand in his pocket while listening to the ring. "Hello, Madeline? Hey, this is Charles," he noticed the quaver in his own voice, "Listen. I need to know what you said to Donna the other day."

"If she didn't tell you, then it's private," the woman clipped.

"Bullshit," he replied sternly, "Look, I don't know what kind of game you're playing with her, but I want it to stop!"

"Oh, you want it to stop?" her tone became filled with anger, "You listen to me. Donna is my daughter! She has been through a traumatic experience."

"Oh, and I suppose being dead for three days doesn't count, so I have no idea what she's been through," he countered.

"This isn't about you!" he held the phone away from his ear as she screamed, "This is about her! She is different Charlie! And not just a little bit!"

"Hey," he tried not to shout, "Keep your voice down, ok? I want what's best for her, an' I don't wanna argue!" Daring to place the device closer to his head, he cursed, "Jesus Christ, woman! You act like you're the only one that cares about her."

"I never said I was the only one," she had lowered her volume, but the rage remained crystal clear, "I said she's a different person."

Charlie caught his breath, her choice of words slapping him in the face. "Different how?" he whispered loudly.

"Everyhow," she pushed her words through clenched teeth. "Her mannerisms, her speech, her food! It's like my baby left her body, and someone else took over!"

Blinking into the darkness, he realized he was short on time, if he wanted the call to remain a secret. "So what did you say to her?"

"Exactly that, Charlie. I've told her, time and again, that she has changed, but she doesn't listen."

"And what did you tell her about dark spirits?" he demanded.

"Dark spirits?" she gasped, "I never said anything… Wait. I said that she was behaving as if she had been possessed…" her voice trailed away. "I'm sorry, Charlie, I didn't mean it that way," her apology sounded genuine. "I was angry. I'm still angry; we see her less and less, and when we do, she's so different."

"Well, I wouldn't know," he sighed loudly. "What I do know, is that she needs me. I have to go. Good night," he clipped, ending the call without waiting for the reply. Returning the phone to the table, he moved to the kitchen, where he began to wash the pans and put the clean dishes away.

Once things were in order, he removed two cups from the cabinet and started a pan of strong tea. "Is that for me?" a small voice interrupted his thoughts from the door.

Lifting his gaze, he stared at the tall blonde who stood in the wide frame that connected the two rooms. Noticing her damp hair still dripped on her robe, he smiled slightly, "Yeah. I thought you might like a nice cup."

"Sure," she stepped closer, her bare feet sticking to the floor as she moved.

"Do you feel better?" his dark eyes were filled with concern below his furrowed brow.

Inhaling deeply, she reached for her mug, dropping in a couple of sugar cubes and locating a spoon. "Actually, I do." Her blue orbs wide, she cut them over at him, "I'm going to tell you about it, Charlie. But you have to promise me not to tell anyone else."

Taking a slow step back, he tightened his jaw, "It's hard to do that before I know what you're gonna say. What if it's something that I *need* to tell someone? I don't wanna make a promise I have t' break."

"It won't be," she assured, turning slowly and taking a seat at the table, "In fact, telling other people could be dangerous."

Pouring his own cup, he joined her, "I'll listen with an open mind, but I can't promise you to keep it a secret." He stared at her blankly, "You have to know I'm worried about you, love."

"I know," she smiled, "And that means so much to me. Please," she indicated the seat he had not yet taken, "Sit and listen. I will do my best to make it clear."

Sinking slowly into the cushioned chair, he watched her features, aware of how unmoved she appeared. *She's always had such a beautiful face.* Lifting his cup, he clasped it with both hands to prevent it from shaking, exposing his fear of whatever it was his lover would reveal.

EIGHTEEN

Make Me Believe

"Ok, I'm ready," he breathed, sipping noisily from the steaming cup.

"Oh, Charlie," she giggled loudly, her smile reaching her sullen eyes and causing them to twinkle, "You look so scared!"

"Do I?" his voice squeaked slightly, and he grinned. "Ok, I'm a little uptight. I'm not sure what you're gonna say t' me."

"Don't be scared, Charlie," her voice deepened. "I'm going to tell you about the first time we met."

He stared, blinking at her for a full minute, "At the airport," he finally conceded. "The time I saw you, on our way to Miami, or the return flight, when you sat next to me?"

"No," she shook her head slowly, "In between that time, we met; but you have forgotten all about it."

Swallowing visibly, he placed his cup to his lips, his mind spinning. "Before my accident?" he supplied.

"After," she did not take her eyes off of him, her glare making him uncomfortable.

"I think I would remember if we had met after. I pretty much went from the hospital to the airport," he shook his head slightly, "We didn't meet, until we were waiting for the plane."

"I need you to listen, Charlie. Don't think about if I'm right or wrong. Just listen; and accept what I am telling you until I get to the end. Then you can try to find the holes in my story," she took a gulp of her tea and waited.

"Ok," he shrugged, "I'll try anyways. You know, finding the holes in things is what I'm best at; I love a good mystery."

"This isn't a mystery," she tucked her foot beneath her and leaned on the flat surface between them. "Although, it can seem like it is. But that's only because there's magic in it." She could see his eyebrows shoot up, and she smiled wryly, "You were hard to convince last time, as well. And this time will be tougher because I no longer have my powers."

"Your powers," he muttered under his breath, no longer able to look her in the eye.

"Yes," she agreed in a soft voice, "I'm going to start at the beginning. I told you, my name is Clarisse. I was born in London, where I lived with my parents - nuh-uh," her hand shot up to cut him off, seeing that he was prepared to interrupt her. "Just listen, baby. When I'm done, then you can ask. I know you will have many questions," she smiled at the memory of the last time she had taught him about her world.

"My parents and I were on board the Titanic, when it sank. My body was lost to the sea. When that happened, I became an angel. A Light Angel; I took care of people, and became their guardian. That's how I met you, that first time; you were my charge. When you were hit by a car, you were rifted, or taken before your time, and it was my job to train you to also be a guardian angel," she paused, sipping from her cup and closing her eyes for a moment.

"But it really wasn't your time," she repeated. "Because of this, Destiny gave you the option; to stay with me, or to return to your family. After our days together, you chose to return. I was happy for you, and wished you well, knowing you would not remember me or any of the things that I had taught you," she could see him beginning to fidget in his chair.

"At the same time, this girl," she indicated herself, "Donna, was on a cruise; a ship that sank. She died, Charlie. It was her time, and Fate claimed her. But Destiny took pity on me; on us really. She allowed me to take this body and to make it my own. She broke our laws, and in doing so, I have crossed from the plane of the Angels to rejoin the world of the Living. This world, love."

Trying desperately to allow her to finish, he exhaled loudly, running his fingers roughly across his lips as if to seal them. Bouncing his legs, he tapped his feet, willing her to hurry so that he could begin his rebuttal.

"So now that we have been together, and I have had my time to walk among the living," her lip began to quiver, "I see that I have placed you in danger. A Dark Angel hunts us. I don't know how; he was claimed by Keeper, and should be dead. But he's here, Charlie. I know that it's him and that he will hurt you if he's able!"

Unable to take it any longer, the young man burst into a twisted laugh at her last juicy tidbit, "A dark angel, huh. You mean a *demon*?" Her eyes grew wide in surprise. "An' you were on the Titanic, which sank. And on a cruise ship, which also sank. Boy, that's a huge coincidence, don't ya think?" he sneered. "Oh, and the best part, you had *magic*, but it's gone now, so you can't do anything all..." he wiggled his fingers in front of him, "All sparkly an' prove it to me."

"That's enough, Charlie!"

"Oh, no," he shook his brown curls at her, "That's not nearly enough. You know what they call this? They don't call it crazy! Oh, no, that's too broad of a term," he held up a single digit in front of her, putting his psychology class to good use, "They call this *paranoid delusional.* That's what this is."

Leaping to his feet, he grabbed their empty cups, turning his back on her and stomping into the kitchen, tossing them in the sink. Leaning over the area with stiff arms, he scowled at the potholders hanging on the wall in front of him. "I want to help you, Donna, I really do - "

"Clarisse," she corrected, cutting him off.

Turning slowly, he faced her, "Clarisse." *Oh my God, she's fucking insane!*

"He's not a demon, he's a Dark Angel. His name is Gous," she supplied, raising her chin slightly as if to challenge him.

Resting his rear end against the edge behind him, "Anything else you'd like to say?" he smoldered.

"Your keys magically appeared in plain sight. Your phone was dead, and then it wasn't. Those are the work of a Light Angel, Charlie. A Summer Angel, changing your environment to give you a push," her voice remained calm.

"Yeah, a Summer Angel, now?" he froze, recalling he had heard that before, "Actually, I gave you that term, last year when we met. I remember you commenting about it at the airport, when we were laughing about our guardian angels working overtime," he glowered.

"Yes, you did, and I was shocked that you said it!" her face lit up, "Where did you hear that, Charlie?"

He blinked at her, confused for a moment. "I don't remember," he shook his head, laying his arms across his chest, "But that means you got it from me."

The girl's laughter tinkled loudly, her smile surprising him with a jolt, "No, baby, you got it from me. From what I taught you. Maybe your memories aren't gone; maybe we just need to find a way to revive them."

Standing up straight, he ran his fingers through his wild curls, sighing loudly. "It's late; I think we need to get some sleep."

"We can't!" she leapt to her feet, "Don't you see? Now that I've told you, we have to finish this! We are in *danger*, Charlie!"

"You know," he chopped the air between them, pointing at her with a stiff hand, "I think your family is right. I think you've become irresponsible. We have work, and we have school, and we have a life we have to take care of. We can't just drop everything and go chasing off after some... fantasy!"

"It's not a fantasy, Charlie!" her hands flew to her hips in disgust.

"I know, you said that, but you also said you can't prove it."

"No, I can't," her lip took on a heavy pout, "That's why it's called *faith*. It's when you take something and believe in it on trust; not because you have proof that it exists."

Inhaling deeply, he could see he wouldn't be getting any rest in his own bed that night. *Unless I can reach her; somehow convince her that she's wrong.* "Ok," he announced, opening his arms wide, "Make me believe."

NINETEEN

Worth Dying For

TURNING ON HER HEEL, Clarisse's robe flowed around her, her feet quick when she took to the stairs, "I need to get dressed, hun! Man, this has been the hardest part to get used to I think..." she disappeared into the bedroom above.

Standing in the living room below, he stared up at the loft, shouting, "What has?"

"Having to do everything by hand," she called, throwing on her shirt and fastening her jeans. Carrying her tennis shoes, she clomped eagerly down the steps, "Used to, I could change clothes in an instant. All I had to do was think about what I wanted to wear," she perched on the ottoman and pulled on her footwear.

"That, and we could travel in the blink of an eye," her smile broad, she continued, "We went all over the world, Charlie. That's how I'm going to show you!"

"I think you need a doctor, Don - Clarisse," he pinched the bridge of his nose as if his head were splitting.

"Trust me," she selected a jacket to combat the evening air, pointing him towards the exit. "One stop, that's all we need, and I can prove it to you."

"Oh, yeah? And how are you going to do that?" he followed, locking their door behind him.

"You're going to follow my lead," she waited by the car, "I'm going to introduce you to one of my old clients. I'm going to tell you the story on the way down, and when we get there, you can ask them about it."

Letting her in the car, his frown grew heavier, "I don' really wanna involve anyone else in this. Unless it's medical help."

"Oh, come on, what's talking to one person going to hurt?"

"GET YOUR HANDS UP!" a male voice commanded loudly, the same instant Charlie felt a hard object pressed into his back.

Raising his appendages slowly, his eyes remained fixed on the girl, who sat in the seat with the open car door between them. "Hey, it's ok, buddy," he called to the man behind him.

"The fuck if it is," the voice growled, hands patting against his body, "Where's your wallet?"

"Uh," the young man looked down at himself, bumping the glass in front of him and causing the door to close, "I guess I left it in the house," he admitted, while trying to see behind him.

Punching him in the back, the bandit knocked him against the parked vehicle, "Whatta you think I am, stupid? Yur drivin' this hunk a shit, where's your license?"

"I told you," Charlie stammered, "I must've left it inside. Look, we were havin' a fight, an' I forgot it, ok?" he turned enough to talk to the man behind him without moving all the way. Judging by the guy's feet, he could see there was at least three or four feet between them, and he had a plan. Slowly turning the fob in his left hand, he drew a deep breath.

In an instant, his thumb hit the lock button, then bounced over to the red panic one. Holding it, he set the alarm off and broke into a dead run, hoping to lead him away from the car, and more importantly, the girl. Realizing at the corner that no one pursued, he stopped and took a look behind him.

About half way between the two locations, the assailant lay on the ground, out cold. Next to him, a late model sedan sat, passenger door wide open. Walking towards him, Charlie was only dimly aware of the alarm that continued to sound, and the people who had begun exiting their front doors to investigate the ruckus.

Regaining consciousness, their attacker rolled onto his knees, giving his head a good shake before reaching for the handle in front of him, and using it to hoist himself to his feet. To his surprise, the action incurred the wrath of the vehicle's owner. "What the hell are you doin' t' my car, man?" their tall, dark-haired neighbor demanded. Rather than respond, the villain took off, sprinting in the opposite direction and disappearing into the dark.

Exiting the still sounding transport, the girl jogged over to her companion, grasping him firmly and removing the keys from his curled digits. Using the button, she silenced the horn and whispered, "It's ok, baby. He's gone."

Turning his head slowly, Charlie drew his gaze away from the direction the man had disappeared. Placing it on the girl who stood next to him, he looped an arm around her, clutching at her thin body and grasping at her scalp, "Oh, my God! What the hell happened?" he breathed in a daze.

"Come inside, dearest," she patted him on the chest, leading him back to their apartment, then closing and locking the door behind them. Helping him out of his jacket, she continued softly, "Gous sent that man to attack us. And we have a guardian angel looking out for us; I'm sure of it."

"How do you know?" he stared at his trembling hands, "He was chasing me; I wanted to get him away from you," the adrenaline still clouded his thoughts.

"I know," she led him up the stairs. "But that car's door opened, right at the precise moment to knock him down. A bold move, and definitely more obvious than a practiced angel would use, but effective."

At the top of the stairs, she stopped, turning to linger so that she would be a few inches taller than the man she loved, "I'm so sorry, Charlie."

"For what?" he exhaled, noting how close her breasts were to his face in the unusual position. Placing his hands upon her, he raised his chin, and she kissed him roughly, guiding him to the landing at the same time.

Pulling at his shirt, she hoisted it over his head, exposing his smooth chest. Her fingers splayed across him, she noted how he had matured, much more man than boy since the first time he had lain with her. "I love you, Charlie," she admitted, tugging at his pants when they had entered their room.

Catching her, he spun her around, planting her against the wall between the door and the dresser, holding her there so he could look her in the eye, "Are you really crazy?" he heaved.

She explored him with agile fingers, "No, baby, I'm not going crazy. They're going to kill us, for what I've done. There is no escape."

"Then what do we do?" he demanded hoarsely.

"Make love to me," she begged, pushing him away and dropping her own tee to the floor. "Please, Charlie. Show me what it's like to be alive, while we still can." Grasping her button, she opened her pants, tossing them next to the shirt, and removing the rest.

His heart still pounding inside his chest, his muddled thoughts could do no other, and he removed the remainder of his own clothing. Eagerly pushing her across their new bed, he sighed loudly, "I always thought you were my angel, baby."

She giggled, "Yes, and you're mine. This could be our last time, Charlie; make it worth dying for..."

TWENTY

Divide the Planes

THE ROOM GLOWED BRIGHTLY when Charlie awoke the following morning. In his arms lay the most beautiful girl he had ever seen. Pulling her nakedness against him, he grinned, nuzzling her neck, "Good morning, Summer Angel." Pushing himself on top of her, he recalled the rough love they had made the night before. He had been with few girls before she came into his life, and he had grown up learning to please her.

Grabbing her hands, he held them over her head, using his legs to part her thighs and find his way inside. She moaned with pleasure at his forcefulness, panting as he drove them to completion. Throwing off the covers when they were finished, he stood next to the bed and extended his hand, "Shower with me?"

"Why not?" she grinned, her body still tingling from the fire he so easily kindled within her.

Once they were clean, they stood beneath the warm spray, allowing the steam to surround them. Gripping her flesh firmly, he kissed her, shifting his grasp to her hair, pulling and then releasing it playfully before cutting off the flow and handing her a fresh towel.

"So, tell me about this Dark Angel," he announced. "You said he was going to kill us. How exactly is he going to do that?"

Wrapping the rough cloth around her, she stepped into their closet between the bedroom and bathroom doors, "I don't really know. He can't attack us directly," she slipped on a pair of silk panties. "That's why he sent the mugger last night."

"Men are his pawns then; like minions," he struggled to gain clarity while tugging his denims into place.

"Something like that," she located her own clothing as well. "I guess I should tell you the rules of magic."

"Only those who are chosen can see it," he stated, tossing his shirt lightly to play with it and causing the muscles in his chest to ripple as he stared at her.

"How did you know that!" she demanded loudly, her mouth hanging open in awe.

Pursing his lips, he continued to gaze at her for a long moment, then pulled the clothing over his head and adjusted it into place. "I've always been different, Clarisse," he stated flatly, "And I've never told a soul about it." Taking his socks and shoes, he descended to the kitchen in search of something to eat.

When she arrived in the wide doorway, she paused, watching him scramble eggs and make toast. Moving to the fridge, she pulled out juice and poured generous glasses for them. She didn't ask, wanting to give him time to adjust to the idea of sharing his deepest secrets with her. Buttering their bread, she used a plate and served herself, taking a seat at the tiny dining table across from him.

Stirring the meal, he admitted quietly, "When I was a little kid, I used to dream that I had a guardian angel. She was a beautiful girl, with long flowing blond hair, like you." She glared at him with wide eyes, aware that he had in fact had one, and that she had been it. "Things used to happen," he explained further, "Crazy things. Simple things. And I dreamed up this girl, who was responsible for them."

Taking a few bites, his mind sifted through the memories. "To be honest, I haven't thought about her in years; not since about seventh grade or so, when I began to grow up I guess."

"You never told me this, when we met on the other side," she blinked at him in disbelief.

"Probably not; I never told anyone. I had become pretty sullen by my later teens, wrapped up in my own little world. That's why everyone thought my near-death experience was so good for me," he chuckled. "Well, two-fold really; my parents fell in love again while I was out, and I learned how to care about other people again."

"Wow," she smiled, "I knew about your parents. You were so concerned about what would become of them if you stayed on the other side."

"The other side," he laughed again, "So tell me about Gous. That's his name, right? Why is he after us?"

"That's a long story, Charlie," she exhaled loudly, reaching for her juice. "The short version is, people who die are supposed to stay dead. Only on rare occasions, when a rifting occurs, are they allowed to return to the living."

"Ok, define rifting."

"We all have our destiny, but sometimes we get caught up in someone else's," she grinned. "When that happens, and you die, we call that rifted. Their fate, not yours. Destiny, head of the Light Angels, grants those people the ability to return, if she chooses, and they come back to this plane."

"If she chooses; she doesn't have to?"

"No, she can refuse."

"An' you said she let you have that body, but she wasn't supposed to."

"Yes," her eyes darted away, uncomfortable with what was coming. "I wanted you so badly, Charlie. I wasn't thinking straight, about what it would do to you, or to Donna's family."

"They knew something wasn't right."

"Sure did," she nodded heavily, "I looked like her, but I couldn't act like her. Of course, you didn't care, because you had no idea who she was before I took over. But everyone else; they knew."

"Yeah, that's what Madeline said; like her daughter was gone, and someone else had taken over her body."

"When did she say that?" the girl's eyes grew wide.

"Last night," he spun his fork in his hand nervously, "I called her while you had your bath. I guess I had already begun to suspect your story was true, even before you had begun to tell it."

Sitting back in her chair, she pushed her empty plate away while she studied him. "How so?"

"Promise you're not gonna get upset?"

Clenching her jaw, she recalled what he said about making blind promises. "Is it something I should be upset about?"

"I dunno," he frowned. "It only started after the accident, an' not right away. I'd say, since Christmas."

"What did!" she demanded loudly, "Come on, quit beating around the bush already." A loud crash immediately followed in the kitchen behind him, causing the girl to jump, panting, "What the hell was that?"

Laying his fork across his plate, he stated quietly, "Maybe you should go find out." Remaining in his chair, he waited for her report.

Returning a moment later, skillet in hand, she mumbled, "This was on the floor. But you already knew that, didn't you. You didn't even flinch at the bang, because you knew it was coming."

"Are you mad?" he asked quietly.

"No," she breathed, reclaiming the chair and laying the pan next to the plates, "But tell me how you did it."

"I don't know how I did it. I told you, it started after Christmas, near as I can tell. I'm still not very good at controlling it, either," his eyes flicked away. "You said last night you used to teleport, and that's when I knew for sure you were telling the truth. I've dreamt several times since the accident that I was in London. You know; poof, in London."

"We did go to London," she sounded out of breath. "I had a client there. What else?"

"I don't know what else," he shrugged his right shoulder, his fingers fidgeting with the edge of his plate. "I think, whatever this Destiny person did, was a lot worse than you realize."

"Oh, no," she took a ragged breath, "What if you're right? Gous is supposed to be dead, but he isn't. You're not supposed to remember anything, but you do. What if giving me this body broke something?"

"How do you mean?" he closed one eye, and glared at her with the other, causing her to laugh.

"Please don't do that, it looks way too creepy!" When he had opened both again, she smiled, "Thank you. I mean, there is supposed to be a clear division between the plane of magic and the plane of the living. I mean like a set in stone dividing line."

"But she blurred it," he finished for her. "Wow, that's deep. And wrong on so many levels. You said he can't attack us directly, but if the planes are no longer divided, who knows what he'll be able t' do."

Standing abruptly, the girl cast a slow glance around her, taking in the room, then staring through the glass panes beside her. "We have to get out of here. We have to fix this."

"Clarisse, I hate to break it to you, but if you're the cause, then you are probably the solution."

"What do you mean?" she turned to glare at him.

"I mean, we have to divide the planes. And to do that… you probably have to go back to the other side."

TWENTY-ONE

Who I Am

"ARE YOU SAYING... I have to die?" Clarisse stared at him with a relaxed jaw.

"Mmm, yeah," he bobbed his head around as if he were a dash ornament, "I mean, it appears obvious. Do you have any idea who we can talk to, on this side of the cosmos?" Standing swiftly, he noted she took a step back from him, "What's the matter?"

Breathing in a deep, slow pant, she stammered, "You're not going to hurt me, are you?"

His brown orbs wide, he glared at her for a long moment, "How could you even think that I would? You're the love of my life, Donna!" he cringed as soon as he said the name, "Or Clarisse, or whatever the hell you wanna call yourself. You," he pointed at her, raking his hand up and down in front of her form, "In there. You, are the half that makes me whole," and the color drained from his face as soon as he said it, "Shit!"

"What?" she clipped.

Tugging at his bangs, he pulled them back and held them out of his face, unsure if she should know. Deciding not to hide the truth, he confessed, "I bought you a ring... with a diamond on it. I was going to give it to you, on vacation this summer."

"Oh my God, are you serious?" she shouted, unable to hide the smile, throwing herself into his arms. "Holy shit, Charlie! You wanna marry me?"

Feeling awkward for a moment, his hands moved about restlessly before he could calm himself. Taking a deep breath, he pushed his arms around her, giving her a firm squeeze, "As a matter of fact, I do. Or I did. I have to admit, in light of the last twenty-four hours, I'll be shocked as hell if I get to."

Leaning back so she could see his face, she continued to grin, "Wow, that's pretty blunt there, Charlie Phillips. I suddenly feel like a vampire, with a human lover who wants to put a stake through my heart."

Her blue eyes dancing, he felt drawn in by her twisted sense of humor. "I do love you," he ran his hand up and down her spine, "So let's see if we can work this out without the stake, ok?" He grinned a little wider, "An' you need to pick; which name are you gonna use?"

Crinkling her nose while she showed him her full set of teeth, she replied, "Clarisse. That's who I am. And if I have to avoid Donna's family until we get this sorted out, all the better."

"Oh, Christ!" he exclaimed, "Donna's family! That's who we need t' go see!"

"Who?" her brow furrowed, "Please don't tell me you want to go see Madeline!"

"Oh, hell no," he spun around, gathering the plates and pan off the table, then carrying them to the sink. "You said Grandma Parker could tell you weren't Donna."

"And?"

"And, we need to pay her a visit, but now, when no one else is around. See what she says. Maybe she's a link to the other side!"

"Wow, Charlie, that's fabulous!" she beamed, helping to clean up their mess.

Climbing into their car a short time later, the couple eagerly drove across town to the nursing home. Holding his hand across the console, Clarisse leaned her head back against the seat, relieved at how things appeared to be working out, "I sure am glad to be getting back to the old me."

"Tired of being human?" he queried.

"Yes, I think that I am, actually. I mean, I dreamed of getting to be alive, pretty much since the day I died. But now that I'm here," she paused, "Well, if it weren't for you, there wouldn't be much here for me to enjoy."

"You miss being an angel," he supplied.

"Yes," she sighed loudly, "I do. It was an important job. I hate to think how many of my clients have been claimed since I stepped down. Oh crap!" she bolted upright in the seat.

"What?" he flicked his gaze over, unable to look at her squarely on the highway.

"Last night, I said we have a Summer Angel looking out for us; but what if we don't? What if all of the things that are happening are you?" she gasped.

"Me?" his voice rose sharply, "Nu-huh; no way. Maybe the car door, but I doubt it. And the phone? Not a chance. Someone or something is doing things, just like when I was a kid."

"You really noticed when you were little?" she tried to hide her disappointment that he had caught on to her antics.

Turning into the center, he showed her his left palm, "Not a whole lot; only a few things. Crazy things, and not necessarily that happened to me. I had a best friend, named Pete. I was riding with him and his dad one day to get ice cream," they climbed out of the car so he paused, guiding her up the steps.

Inside the elevator, he continued, "So we get our cones, and his dad is driving, while trying to eat his. We're stopped at a red light, an' he's lickin' away at it. When the light turns green, the car behind us honks, an' he stops to look up at the light, an' I swear to God, the scoop hops off the cone and falls in between his legs," he used his hands to demonstrate for her, causing her to frown.

"So, instead of moving, he's looking at his lap, and a semi runs the red light, an' smashes into the car that had been beside us. They took off when the guy honked, an' we didn't," he finished as the doors opened.

Staring at him with wide eyes, "You saw the ice cream fall?"

"Yeah, it was amazing! It looked like it was alive and literally jumped off," he grinned.

Arriving in front of the correct door, she caught his arm, "I never knew that you suspected," she breathed. "If I had, I probably would have lost you as a client. Maybe even been pulled from duty; it's really hard to say."

"Why? Is revealing the other plane against the rules?" he grinned at her.

"It is," she nodded vigorously, "So be careful in here, Charlie. I don't know what they would do to you, if you tell her anything, but I would rather not find out."

"I'll keep that in mind," he slid his arms around her waist, "And thank you for not letting a truck run over us that day."

"You're welcome, baby," she grinned, giving him a quick kiss, then reaching for the door.

TWENTY-TWO

The Other Side

INSIDE THE TINY SUITE, Grandma Parker's chair sat by the window. Perched inside of it, the elderly woman stared out across the park below, watching the birds come and go. Stepping further in, the girl called tentatively, "Hello?"

"Why, hello!" her caretaker replied from the tiny kitchen area, cup towel in hand, "What a surprise, Grandma! Look who's here to see you!"

Moving across to greet her, Clarisse knelt down, a warm feeling in the pit of her stomach. *It's ok that she doesn't know me,* she rationalized. *In fact, it's great that she doesn't.* "Hey, how are you?"

Smiling, the other woman addressed Charlie, "Are you going to be here long?"

"A while," he grinned back at her, "We'll let you know at the desk when we leave if you like."

"Sure, I can take my break, thanks!" Dropping her rag on the counter, she exited and closed the door softly behind her.

As soon as she was gone, Grandma perked up, "I was wondering if you would come by."

Her mouth gaping, Clarisse stood straight up, "Oh, you were!" Her eyes darting over at her companion, she clasped her hands in front of her, "Were you expecting me to?"

The smile faint, it gave the woman's features an odd appearance, causing Charlie's chest to grow tight. Closing the distance, he instinctively grasped Clarisse's arm, guiding her away from the seated figure.

"Oh, protective now, are we," her voice had grown deeper, no longer sounding like a sweet old lady.

"Gous!" the girl shrieked, "You're not allowed to possess a living being!"

"Neither are you," he quipped, still manipulating his puppet.

"Donna was dead," the girl hissed, "It's not the same."

"Still against the rules," a shoulder shrugged. "I have a message for you," he paused, the grey eyes cutting over at Charlie, "It's from Keeper."

"From Keeper!" she inhaled sharply, "What does he say?"

"He says he doesn't blame you… for this situation," a hand raised to indicate her present form. "But, it must be rectified, none the less. You must cross over, and return to the plane in which you belong, Summer Angel."

"Just her, or both of us?" Charlie interrupted him for clarification.

"Not you," Gous spoke through his disguise, "The girl." Cutting his gaze over to her, the smile on his lips appeared positively wicked. "You have one day to complete the task."

"How?" she didn't even flinch. "I'm sure there are good ways and bad ways to go about it."

Raising a hand, a wrinkled finger pointed at the bathroom, "Look in the medicine cabinet, child," the old woman's voice was her own for the moment, causing the girl to shudder.

Slipping into the other room, she opened the cabinet, and knew immediately what he referred to. Lifting the small brown bottle, it held no label, and was topped with a white dropper bulb. She held it out through the doorway so the Grandmother Gous could see it, "This one?"

"Yes, that one," Gous growled again. "Three drops. Put it in your tea; take a nice long nap," his laughter rumbled, "I'll see you on the other side, Clarisse."

"Wait!" Charlie called, afraid he would leave before they had all their answers, "This will fix everything, right?"

"This will repair the damage between the planes, yes," their source provided.

"And what if she decides not to go," he played the devil's advocate.

The old woman's features became distorted, a snarl forming on her lips, "She will go, one way or another. The only question is, who will be going with her!"

His threat clear, the young man swallowed hard, "All right," he issued a small wave, "Can we talk to Grandma now?"

In an instant, the frail body fell limp in the seat. "Grandma!" Clarisse screamed, "Charlie, get the nurse!"

Dashing from the room, he arrived at the counter out front a moment later, "Please, help!" he panted, "She fainted!" being the only explanation he could give. Returning to the small apartment, he discovered the girl, kneeling in front of the old woman, who looked up with pale blue eyes when he came in.

"Oh, she's ok!" he sheepishly stepped aside to let the nurse in behind him.

"Yes, it was crazy," Clarisse stood, wringing her hands, "One minute she was talking, then she was out, then she was awake again!" She turned to her caretaker, "Does she do this often?"

"No, she's never done it before," the practiced hands assessed her vitals, "Are you feeling ok, Grandma?"

"Yes, I'm fine," the raspy voice stated, leaving the couple in awe.

"Maybe we should go," Charlie suggested while reaching for his girl-friend's hand. "We'll come again another time," he lied straight up, knowing they had no intention of ever returning.

TWENTY-THREE

Magic Touch

INSIDE THEIR VEHICLE and headed for home, the couple relaxed into the quiet. Lost in thought, Charlie's mind worked overtime, trying to figure out how they could get more information, at one point stating aloud, "I have a real problem going off of what Gous had t' say."

"Me too," the girl next to him sighed, watching the stripes zip by her window on the asphalt below. "He's a Dark Angel, so by nature a liar and a wicked being. To believe that Keeper would trust him with anything is difficult to fathom."

"But, then again," he tacked on, "You did say Keeper destroyed him. The fact that he was there would indicate that's not true. We need more information, plain an' simple." Taking their exit, he placed his elbow on the glass, noting the fuel gauge, "We gotta have gas."

Pulling into the station, filling the tank was a quick and easy process; *it only holds nine gallons,* he smiled to himself. Recalling what he had learned about them before he chose the vehicle, he knew that a hybrid is the best of both worlds. *It can use two kinds of energy, basically passing between the two seamlessly to make the most of the resources available.*

The idea rolling around in his head, he began to draw a comparison, *like the two planes.* The plane of the living is physical, and the plane of magic, where the angels reside. *I guess that makes me a hybrid.* The idea gave him a small fit of giggles before it morphed into a type of epiphany.

"Has anyone in this plane ever used magic before?" he demanded when he slid back into the driver's seat.

Turning to gape at him, Clarisse stammered, "Not that I have ever heard of. There have been many living that claimed to have power, but none that were authentic to my knowledge."

"I guess that means I have the magic touch," he chuckled, starting the car and pulling away. "Still, I want to contact someone on the other side, and not Gous. You said there was a Summer Angel looking out for us; we need to get in touch with him."

"That's not possible, Charlie," she sighed, "The planes are divided."

"Right, but why are they divided, hmm?" he flicked a quick glance at her, and answered his own question, "Because it's against the rules for Angels to reveal themselves, and the living don't know about them. But we do. You and I are both hybrids; part of both worlds, like this car." Seeing her confusion, he gave her a quick rundown on how the vehicle uses two types of energy.

"That's pure genius," she breathed, in genuine awe of his discovery.

"Not really," he shrugged, "What we need t' do is figure out how t' make it possible for him to talk to us. I assume he can hear what we say, yes?"

"Yes, he can hear."

"But he can't reply."

"No," she shook her long tresses, "He can talk to others in his plane, but not to us."

"So, how did you move the ice cream? Is it like what I did with the pan?" he pulled the car to the curb, a few doors down from their apartment.

"Pretty much," she confessed. "We can use our powers to move or manipulate things when we choose to, but otherwise we pass through, especially people. We don't really exist in a physical sense."

Climbing out and darting around between traffic, he met her with a huge grin, "You know, I heard a story once about a bus load o' kids that died in a train wreck. I don't remember the town, but if you park your car on the tracks, they will push it outta the way."

"That's nonsense," she rolled her eyes and stepped inside, closing the door behind her. "One of the main rules is to remain hidden; nothing obvious. They wouldn't push a car out of the way, especially if people were in it."

"But you could do it, if you wanted to," he insisted.

Shrugging, she acquiesced, "Sure, I suppose that you could, but then the people in the car wouldn't get it; it's part of the protection. Any time you hear about something caused by supernatural forces, it probably wasn't. People don't see magic, Charlie. So what are you thinking here?"

"In the story, you're supposed to put baby powder on your bumper, and their handprints show up from pushing the car," he replied over his shoulder while darting into the kitchen. Following, she observed while he searched their cabinets. Removing a small bag of flour, he grinned. Using a knife, he punctured it, scattering it across the floor.

"What the hell are you doing!" she shrieked, "That's going to be one hell of a mess to clean up, and I told you; angels pass through objects. If you think you'll get footprints or anything, you're wasting your time!"

"I don't really care about footprints," he chewed on his bottom lip, surveying the project, "But, he could make marks in it, if he wanted to."

"I suppose," she tossed up her hands in exasperation. "So what kind of marks do you think he would want to make?" she huffed at his refusal to understand.

"I dunno," he shrugged, "I think he could use it like a chalkboard if he wanted."

"Well, first off, I have only speculated that we have a guardian angel; I don't really know that for sure. Destiny would have to assign us one; unless someone has picked us up, and I doubt that would have happened," her eyes narrowed slightly.

"Why do you sound angry?" he dropped his half empty bag on the counter. "We need t' get this information, and this is a way we might be able to do it. And besides, Destiny put you in that body. You don't think she would have given you some protection?"

"I don't know that she would have," Clarisse lowered her voice,

"And I guess this is as good a plan as any, at this point." Casting her gaze around the room, she sighed loudly. "So what is it you want to know?"

"What do you mean?" he blinked at her.

"Let's pretend he's here, watching this. You have his attention, at least hypothetically, so what is it you want him, or her, to divulge?"

"Well," he stroked his chin, "I guess the first thing would be to identify himself, so we know who we're dealing with."

"Ok, what else?"

"And, what's the solution? Was Gous tellin' the truth?"

"Fair enough; is that all?"

Charlie appeared thoughtful for a long moment before going further. "Yeah, I guess that it is. At least for the moment," he grasped her hand, "Wonder if he'll respond or if we need to give him some privacy."

"I like how you assume our angel is male," she giggled, tugging him towards the door. "I'm hungry; let's leave her alone so she can give us her message, and get something to eat."

The couple passed through Father, the oldest of the Light Angels, on their way out, as he stood in the dining area so he could observe them. Gliding towards the kitchen, he surveyed the mess the young man had made, commenting aloud, "Clever lad."

"Not clever enough," Gous hissed, coming out of the shadow. "You should never have gotten involved in this, old man."

"You may be right about that," the ancient angel agreed, "But Clarisse and Charlie are in my charge." He waggled a finger at the Dark Angel. "Go, and let me handle this."

"Not a chance," the dark lips parted into a sneer, revealing pointed teeth. "I want to see what you will tell them; in case I need to wipe it away."

"There will be no wiping, minion. We serve the same master, and my message will align with the truth. Be gone, so that I may decide and choose my words with care. Your idle prattle is distracting."

Gous chortled at the insult, "Very well, have your say. The clock is ticking," he turned, dropping his dark hood over his head before he disappeared.

"What a mess," Father muttered, turning back to Charlie's powder covered floor. "Things would have been much simpler if you had remained among the angels, Mr. Phillips." Of course, it had been Clarisse and Destiny's plotting that had put things out of kilter.

Moving closer, he held an arm suspended in the air. Straightening an index finger, he used it to focus, dragging it through the air and using his power to trace the letters. When he had finished, he dropped the hand to his side, a loud sigh escaping the sorrow that plagued his heavy heart.

TWENTY-FOUR

Charlie's Angel

OUTSIDE THEIR TINY APARTMENT, Charlie placed Clarisse into the passenger seat and closed the door firmly. Making it around to the other side and being careful to dodge the traffic, he slid behind the wheel. "I love how we are close to the school and everything, but I'm not sure this was the best street to be on," he muttered, watching his blinker flick while he waited for the right spot to pull out.

Watching him, Clarisse recalled his story about her solution to the accident she had helped his friend's father avoid over a decade before. When he had safely merged, she inquired, "How did you know that your guardian angel was a tall girl with blond hair?"

Keeping his eyes on the road, he grinned, "I saw her."

"You saw her!" she gasped, "That's impossible. I was your guardian angel," she stabbed herself in the chest with a stiff digit, "And I was in the other plane; the magical plane. There is no way you could have seen me."

"I don't care where you were," he turned into a parking lot and found a spot, "I saw you, and more than once I might add. Of course, like I said, I was young, and I don't remember seeing you or anything unusual after I started junior high. But before that... yeah, I knew you were there."

"Ok, tell me how."

Exiting the vehicle, he made his way around to open her door and offered her his hand. Closing it after she stood beside him, he looped his arm around her to guide her inside, "Promise me you won't be upset."

"I promise; it's in the past. But I need to know."

Inside the cafe, he slid into a booth across from her and sighed, "I saw you lots of times; only you weren't solid," he knocked on the table between them, "Almost like I could see through you, and no one else ever noticed you, so I kept it to myself. Then, one time in particular, and come to think of it, probably the last time, I had been really sick. I was laying in my bed, and I told my mom that my angel was watching me, and everything was gonna be ok. She laughed at me and called you *Charlie's angel.*"

"Your mother was so upset," the girl recalled, "She thought you were going to die."

"But you saved me," he grinned brightly.

"No, Charlie, I didn't. That's not really how it works. Destiny and Fate, they more or less control when a person will die, unless you get rifted. It wasn't your time," she shook her long blond strands slightly, "I knew you were going to pull through, but I couldn't drag myself away. You were so special to me, from the moment you were born."

She drew a deep breath, looking around at the other patrons nervously as she admitted, "I watched so closely while you were growing up; almost too closely. After you got better, I realized I needed to step away. I stopped following you as much and gave you plenty of room."

"Why? Were you not my Guardian Angel after that?"

Staring at him with blue eyes wide like saucers, her bottom lip began to tremble. "No, baby. I felt like I had become too attached; I wanted something that I was never meant to have," she took a ragged breath. "It's the reason that I agreed to take Destiny's offer, which has brought us to a bad place."

"No it hasn't!" he countered almost angrily, "This may not be ideal, but I wouldn't trade it for anything!" He glared at her, seeing that his meaning remained unclear. Lowering his voice, he tried again, "I love you; you are the person I was meant to be with. For how long is the real trick; maybe this is all the time we were meant to have."

Staring at him, she blinked back her tears, "So, if I really have to go, you won't be upset?"

"Oh, I'll be upset," he straightened himself in his seat. "I don't wanna lose you. But," he frowned heavily, "I'm thankful for the time we had. I have no regrets, an' wouldn' change the days I've spent with you, either way."

"Oh, Charlie," she sobbed, overcome with a mixture of happiness and grief, "I'm so glad, too. No matter what happens to me, I'm glad we got the chance..." her voice trailed away.

Selecting a menu, he nodded, "Well, now that we got that out of the way, let's quit worrying about the things we can't change."

Plucking a plastic coated card for herself, she sniffed loudly, "I suppose you're right." Placing their orders a few minutes later, they settled into a strained silence, the weight of the future heavy upon them, regardless of how badly they wanted to push it aside.

The sun had set by the time the couple arrived home. Letting them inside, Charlie dashed ahead of her, leaving her to close and lock the front door while he trotted into the kitchen to see if there had been any contact from the other side. Stopping in the wide door frame that connected the two rooms, his breath caught in his chest.

"Son of a bitch," he muttered, staring at the three little words etched in the clumps of flour. As the girl stepped up behind him, he swung his right hand through the air, sending the fine powder spewing into an angry cloud around them.

"Charlie!" she exclaimed, "What did you do that for?"

Ignoring her, he commanded, "Leave it! Let's go to bed, an' we'll worry about that tomorrow." Clasping her fingers, he checked the front door on the way by and led her up the stairs to their bed.

TWENTY-FIVE

Calculated Risk

L<small>YING</small> in the early morning light, Clarisse ran her fingers across the bare shoulder and arm before her. The couple had made passionate love, deeper than the night before, and she had slept soundly beside him afterwards. Being the first awake, she toyed with his naked frame, and the idea of rousing him.

Deciding to allow him to sleep, she scooted closer and draped her arm across him. *It was a calculated risk, taking this body and crossing into this world,* she admitted to herself in the darkness. Unfortunately, the consequences had caught up to them, and she knew in a few hours she would have to make her choice. Holding him tightly, she joined him in his peaceful slumber.

Charlie awoke to the sound of his phone chiming downstairs. Stretching, he scrunched his eyes tightly to hold out the glare, then lay still and listened to the silence. *Wonder who that was.* A few minutes later, the ringtone sang out again, and he leapt out of the sheets and headed to the living room to find out.

Snatching the device off of the charger, he blinked at the name, then pressed the green button, "Hello, Madeline," he glanced down at his naked body and started up the stairs.

"Charlie!" she exclaimed, "Where's Donna?"

"Still asleep," he groaned, "What do you want?"

"I want to speak to my daughter, that's what!" she quipped. "We have an emergency, and her phone goes straight to voicemail. I've been trying to reach her for hours!"

"All right, hold on," he grimaced, holding the cell out to the girl. "It's your mother," he mouthed at her questioning gaze, before realizing the inaccuracy of that statement with a half grin.

Taking it, Clarisse adjusted the bedding to cover herself more fully, "Yes?"

"Donna! We need you at the hospital, right away!" the other woman snapped.

"Why? What's going on?"

"You're grandmother has had a spell, and we need you here," Madeline demanded more firmly.

"What kind of spell?" the girl persisted, pouting slightly.

"Not over the phone," the other woman's tone dropped, "Come to the nursing home, and we will fill you in when you get here."

Removing the device from her ear, the girl blinked her blue eyes at it in disgust. "She hung up. They want us to go to the nursing home; something has happened to Grandma Parker."

"That's not good," he replied, looking around for clothing, then thinking better of it. "Let's grab a quick shower, and get over there."

"I don't want to go," she replied, climbing out of the bed.

"You don't really have a choice. You're still Donna to everyone else, and you have t' play that through." Stepping into the smaller room, he kicked on the shower. "Besides, we have to find out what's going on, in case Gous is going to make good on his threat an' start hurting people since you decided not to off yourself."

"Gous can't do that," she explained, "He can influence someone to give in to primitive desires, using them to do his bidding. But attacking directly is against the rules."

"The rules before you crossed the plane," he stated matter-of-factly while testing the spray. "We have to see what's going on over there, regardless." He climbed into the tub, and she followed as he continued,

"Your time is going to be up any minute, and I'm really scared of what he's gonna do when you don't drink your poison."

Pressing her nakedness against him beneath the warm cascade, she smiled, "I haven't decided what I'm going to do, Charlie. But I want you to know, I love you, either way."

"I know," he returned her grin, "But I'm hoping we can riddle this out an' I get to keep you."

"Unlikely," she switched places and lathered her sticky flesh. "What message did you find in the flour last night?"

Staring at her, he had forgotten all about it. Blowing air slowly through pursed lips, he made a low whistle; *damn.* "It said…" his voice trailed away, and he recalled that *I love you* were rumored to be the hardest three little words to say. *So much for that,* he frowned slightly, "It doesn't matter what it said. I don't think it was from a Summer Angel. I think Gous was listening and tampered with it."

"Well, I can't be sure until you tell me," she reached for a towel, "So let's have it. What did it say?"

"*Let her die,*" his voice cracked as he wrapped himself as well. "I told you, I think that's Gous talking."

"Let her die? That's it?"

"Yeah, that's all it said. And since that's not really what I asked, I think it's bogus," he exited the room to dress and put an end to his discomfort. Once they were decent, the pair descended and climbed into their car. "The nursing home, right?" he finally spoke again, noting that she had remained silent and appeared deep in thought.

"Yes," she agreed quietly, watching the traffic rushing past.

Once they were out on the highway, he reached and took her hand, "I'm gonna support you, no matter what you decide," he could feel his gut wrench as he spoke. *Hell, I may even join you,* he silently added.

"It won't be an easy choice," she turned to look at his profile. "I want you to have a great life, regardless of how this ends."

"I know," he squeezed her digits. Stroking her gently with his thumb, they rode the rest of the way in silence, pondering what might lay ahead.

TWENTY-SIX

What Lies Beyond

WHEN THE COUPLE entered the small chamber, they had no idea what to expect. Opening the wide portal and holding it for the girl, Charlie inhaled deeply in an attempt to steady his nerves. Making his way in behind, he could see that the sitting room was packed with many of the same people who had been there only a few days before.

Shoving his hands in his pockets, he held his chin up in defiance as Madeline grabbed Clarisse and hugged her tightly. When the embrace grew long, he swung his glare around at the others, their dark expressions conveying more than words ever could; *Grandma Parker's dead,* he concluded. His eyes making it back to the women before him, he noted they had both begun to cry.

Raising a gentle hand, he traced the line of his lover's back, "Hey, hey, it's ok," he soothed.

"It's ok?" Donna's mother demanded sharply, standing up straight and pushing the girl away. "We want to know what happened. The nurse said the two of you were here, yesterday. Then, last night, she went from stable to coma in a matter of minutes; only hours after you left, in fact."

Charlie met her accusing glare evenly, unwilling to divulge anything out of hand. Reaching for Clarisse's fingers, he linked them with his before he replied coolly, "We didn't do anything to her, if that's what you mean. We came for a visit. We thought if we came more often, she might remember Donna better," he flat out lied, and the blonde sidled closer to him. "Is that a crime?"

"Maybe," she angrily challenged, "The nurse also said she had some kind of spell while you were here, but it was over before she could assess her. What happened then?"

"Nothing, mother," Clarisse hijacked the confrontation, "She fainted, that's all. It happened and then it was over, that quick!" she snapped her fingers to demonstrate. "I loved Grandma Parker the same as everyone else," she, too, concealed the truth, "And if I thought it was serious, I would have pushed the issue."

"Loved?" her mother blinked at her. "Loved? She's still alive, Donna. Whatever you gave her wasn't enough to kill her; she's tough, even if her mind is a bit stretched."

"Gave her!" Clarisse gasped, drawing a quick conclusion, "You think we did something to her? That we would have harmed her? Poisoned her?" The older woman made no reply, and simply shifted her gaze to the man beside her.

"Hey, you know, I wouldn't have or never would do anything t' harm another person," he wafted a hand in front of him. "So why don' you quit playing detective, an' tell us what the hell is going on."

Madeline's cheeks sucked in as she puckered, her eyes narrowed in an angry scowl, "Now you listen to me, you little weasel. I told you before, there is no place for you! Donna has been through a traumatic experience; she's distraught. But one day, she will get over it, and her life will return to normal. And when that happens, you will be gone."

Inhaling sharply, Charlie prepared to make his retort, but Clarisse cut him off by holding up her hands, "Stop it, both of you! This isn't the time to fight over what either of you think about who I am, or what I need," she darted her eyes between them. "Can I *please* see my grandmother?"

"You may go in," the woman stepped aside, "But he's not welcome."

"That's fine," Charlie huffed, "I'll be in the hall, baby," he called as she disappeared into the small bedroom. Turning his back on Donna's family, he could feel their stares as he exited, as if they would set his back ablaze with only the animosity they held for him.

Inside the second chamber, Clarisse blinked into the dimly lit room. Once her eyes had adjusted, she moved slowly towards the bed and gripped the railing tightly. Listening to the hiss of the machine attached to the mask, she could see the elderly woman's chest rise and fall in rhythm to the sound. "Ok, Gous, I'm here," she whispered loudly, unsure if he would reply.

When the eyes opened, they glowed like warm honey, taking the girl's breath away, "So, you have returned. Didn't take your medicine yet, I see."

"No," she confessed, "Not yet. I'm not sure if that's the best way."

"It's the only way, Summer Angel," his voice rasped. "You will come back to this side, or others will suffer. Many others, starting with that Dark Angel you've taken up with."

"Dark Angel," she gasped. "What are you talking about? Charlie is no such thing as a Dark Angel!"

"Of course he is," the wrinkled lips smiled behind the plastic cover, "You are blinded by your feelings for him."

"You lie!" she hissed, her eyes narrowed, but she had seen the signs and fear sent her heart beating wildly. "You wrote the message to him, didn't you!"

"No," Gous sneered, "Those were Father's words to you."

"Father!" she breathed in disbelief. Her mind leapt to the oldest of the light angels, her entire world suddenly spinning out of control. "Father is in this... with you?" her voice had all but vanished.

"Keeper sent us to make things right; to punish the guilty and put things in order. The planes must be repaired, and your fate awaits you on the other side."

"Oh, no," a tear rolled down her cheek, "Please, promise me that you will spare Charlie! Promise me that he will not be judged for what I've done!" she sobbed loudly, "He's not a Dark Angel, I swear it! Allow him to go on, and have the life that should have been his."

"You have one hour to complete your task; after that, we will destroy him," the eyes closed, and the room slipped back into silence, only broken by the sound of the machines.

TWENTY-SEVEN

Going Home

CLARISSE EXITED THE BEDROOM, walking straight through the crowded space without making eye contact with anyone. She could hear Donna's mother calling after her, only causing her to move faster as she caught Charlie's hand and dragged him after her. Inside the elevator, she waited for the doors to close, and then leaned against the wall, sobbing.

"What happened?" he demanded quietly, resting his hand upon her shoulder. "Did you talk to Gous?"

"Yes," she replied crisply. "It's over Charlie. We have to go home, and you can make me tea, like you did before. I will use the drops, and go to sleep, like he said."

"No," he demanded sharply, a moment before the doors opened and she left him standing alone. Pausing for an instant, he felt lost, as if her words could crush him completely. Moving quickly, he caught up to her as she slid into the driver's seat of their car. "What the hell are you doing?" he shouted.

"I'm going home, Charlie. I have to finish this, once and for all. Get in and go with me if you want, or stay here. In fact, maybe you should stay here. That way, there won't be any question of your involvement."

"Question of my involvement!" he bellowed as she slammed the door in front of him. Darting around to the other side, he climbed into the passenger seat, "Baby, listen; I know you wanna do what's right—"

"I thought you were going to support my choice," she sniffed, starting the car and backing out of the spot.

Charlie gaped at her, watching as she exited the parking lot and pulled onto the freeway. Swallowing a few times, his gut ached as if he had a large stone sitting in the bottom of it. Eventually, he admitted, "I thought I could, but I can't! I can't bear the thought of losing you," he sighed.

"I know, love. But I have to do what's right. They are going to make you suffer, if I don't."

"Then let them," he pleaded.

"No; you don't understand. They aren't going to do anything to you directly. They'll go after your family, Charlie. Your mom; your dad. Things will happen to them."

"You mean, they are going to kill my parents if you don't do this?" his eyes grew wide in disbelief.

"I don't think so, baby. I think they are going to hurt them. You know, there are worse things than dying."

"Worse things? Like what?"

"Imagine if they were to burn them, like in a fire; only, they didn't die. They would suffer miserably, and you would be there to watch. We would have to take care of them, and every day be reminded of why it had happened."

"Stop it! That's not going to happen, and you know it!" he challenged, "You can't let them do this, Clarisse! You can't let them win!"

"They already won, Charlie. They won the moment I crossed the plane," she whispered, easing their car into the parking spot in front of their home. *If he becomes a Dark Angel, it will be because I drove him to it,* she sighed.

"Please, Clarisse," he spoke more quietly, turning in his seat to beg, "We could leave. Go somewhere far away, and then there wouldn't be any reason for them to hurt... anyone."

"They would find us, hun. There is nowhere we could hide," she watched the cars shooting past in the small mirror to her left. "I'm sorry for the pain that I have brought you. I swear to you, if I had known it would end like this..." her voice trailed away.

"It's not over," he begged, tears welling and spilling over from his soft brown orbs, "I love you, Clarisse. Please don't leave me."

Turning her gaze to meet his, she smiled, "I'll always be with you, love. I swear to you, there will be nothing to keep me from following you, all the days of your life. Promise me you will make a good one for yourself."

"Oh my God," his Adam's apple slid up and down as he swallowed, droplets of sorrow dripping unchecked from his jaw, "Oh my God, I hate you! You can't leave me! What am I gonna do without you?" his mind shifted to his ring, and all the plans he had made for their perfect lives together; dreams that would never be fulfilled.

"Don't say that, Charlie. You don't hate me; and someday, you'll forgive me. Please, remember that I love you." She could see him grinding his teeth, and her resolve ebbed for an instant. Her eyes darting to the mirror, she saw her chance to exit. Grabbing the handle, she swung the door wide.

Charlie turned to watch, the blond strands flying out behind her in slow motion as if it were a movie playing out before him, "NO!" he bellowed an instant before the delivery truck made impact, taking off the door of the car in the same instant her body was sent careening down the road to land a few hundred feet in front of them. Trapped in the moment, the only sound he heard was her shoe as it landed noisily on the roof of the vehicle above him.

Charlie stared at the casket, warm sun beating down on his brown hair. Clenching his teeth, he fought the urge to cry; *not here, out in the open.* A moment later, his sorrow got the better of him, and a few fresh tears rolled down his cheek. *Well, that's great.*

He had cried pretty much non-stop from the moment he had watched the woman he loved take her own life. *I couldn't tell them that, though.* He had insisted it had been an accident to anyone who would listen, especially the police; and Donna's mother. He might not have liked the woman, but not enough to add to her pain by allowing her to blame herself for Donna's passing.

The service came to an end, and he made his way over to lay his hand on top of the dark wood. Ready to say his goodbye, before it was lowered into the ground, he breathed deeply and soaked in the golden rays.

Only giving the girl's mother a cursory nod, he turned on his heel and walked away, his parents trailing after him. Climbing into the back seat of his parents' car, he sighed heavily. "You guys are going home, right?"

"We really think you should go home with us, son," his father spoke softly, starting the engine and pulling away.

"I can't," Charlie stared out the window. "There's still a few weeks left in this semester, and I have to finish. I'll come home after finals and spend the summer there, if you want."

The couple exchanged a glance, but said nothing else. Arriving at the townhome, they allowed him to go inside before his mother prodded, "Maybe we should stay another night."

"No, mom. Please; just go home," he sighed loudly. "Really, I'd rather be alone." Making his way up the stairs, he felt grateful the bedroom had a door so that he could close it, and have a few minutes to himself.

Watching him, John nodded, "We need t' go home, Beth. He'll be ok, and I think our being here is only making it worse, somehow."

"I don't know," she sighed, "But I don' know what else to do, either." Gathering their things, she placed their bags beside the door, then called to the loft above them, "We're heading out, Charlie! Come an' give your momma a hug!"

Lying on his bed, turning a small brown bottle of liquid in his hand, he gave the white bulb a squeeze while he exhaled noisily. Getting to his feet, he shoved it into his pocket, and made his way downstairs. "I'll call you guys in a few days," he lied while giving each of them a hug.

"And we'll call tonight, so you know we made it home safe," she forced a smile. "Take care of yourself, baby. I know it hurts, but time heals all things."

"Yeah," he agreed, opening the door as if to shoo them out. "Ok, tonight, but if I don't answer, jus' leave me a message. I have class early, an' may be asleep," he stared at the floor as he spoke.

"Sure, honey. You get some rest," she reached up to push his bangs to the side.

"Beth," John called softly, tugging on her arm. Following obediently, they placed their bags in the trunk of the car, and climbed inside, mindful of the traffic as they moved.

Once the vehicle had rolled out of sight, Charlie closed the door and lay his head against the wooden frame; *please forgive me.* Making his way into the kitchen, he pulled out a pan and filled it with water, then placed it on the stove. Extracting the brown bottle from his pocket, he set it on the counter and gave the bulb another half-hearted squeeze.

Turning to the cabinet, he located the tea bags, and began opening them, one by one, when he heard the sound of a small crash behind him. Spinning with a jump, he glared at the barren surface, and then lowered the gaze to take in the liquid oozing out onto the floor from the shards of dark glass; *shit.*

Kneeling, his thoughts darted to how he might preserve a few drops of the precious liquid; *I don't need much.* Then his mind halted, his hand hanging over the mess for a moment, before he stood up slowly and looked around the empty room.

"Oh my God!" he cried aloud as a smile crept across his face. Standing in awe for a moment, he plopped the bags into his pan of boiling water, then he located a towel and cleaned up the mess. Tossing the rag, glass and all, into the trash, he pulled out a mug and added a few cubes of sugar before pouring in the hot liquid.

Placing the cup on the table, he opened a few cupboards, in search of the half-bag of flour. Before sitting in a chair, he slung the bag side to side several times, allowing the powder to coat the floor before him. Leaning back in his seat, he propped his right ankle onto his left knee and lifted the warm brew, a smile on his lips as he waited, confident the words would come.

PART III
Forgotten Angel

Prologue

"HOLY SHIT!" Charlie clapped his hands over his face, blocking his view of the ceiling above him. Panting heavily, his pulse pounded in his ears. Slowly pulling them down, his palms slid roughly over his stubble coated cheeks.

"This cannot be happening!" he muttered into the darkness, while his mind raced over the images from his dream. *Clarisse;* the thought of her brought pangs of agony. "Baby, are you here?" he called tentatively, knowing a reply would be unlikely.

Clarisse had died only a few short weeks before, having leapt from their car to be struck by a passing truck. To everyone else, it had been an unfortunate accident, but Charlie knew better. *She killed herself,* he sobbed, knowing she had no choice; *she did it to protect me.* Clenching his fists, he fought to regain his outward calm.

Tossing back the blanket, the young man wiped at his drops of sadness angrily; *why the fuck are you still crying over her?* Stumbling into the bathroom, he leaned against the wall for a moment before facing the toilet. "Because I can," he shot back. *And because knowing she's here only makes it worse.*

His fingers lightly trailing the railing on the stairs a few minutes later, he made his way to the kitchen and flicked on the light. Squinting at the brightness, he half smiled at the message etched in the flour covered floor; *yup; she's still here.*

Hey baby, I miss you, but it will be ok, it read.

Swiping his hand through the air above the coating, he used his new magical powers to smooth it and moved to the fridge to pull out a jug of orange juice. "It's getting stronger," he spoke to her aloud, and poured a glass of the cold liquid while trying to ignore the movement below him.

I know, the invisible finger traced.

"I dreamed of you again," he continued, moving to a chair at the table in the dining area that lay between the kitchen and living room. Taking a seat, he once again erased her words. "I'm going home the day after tomorrow. Are you coming with me?"

Yes.

"I'll have to figure out a different system then," he chuckled aloud, "I'm sure my mom ain't gonna want flour all over her kitchen floor while I'm there."

A line appeared under her reply, causing him to smile a little more broadly. Only moments before the accident, Clarisse had promised Charlie she would follow him all the days of his life. At the time, he had thought that was a good thing. Four weeks later, he wasn't so sure; *not that I'm going to tell her that,* he sighed to himself.

TWENTY-EIGHT

Tempted

CHARLIE SLID behind the wheel of his tiny hybrid, only flicking a quick glance at the passenger seat. Adjusting himself in and fastening his seat belt, he watched the traffic over his shoulder until the coast was clear, and he could pull out. "Sure feels weird having the car back," he commented aloud.

The damaged door had been replaced, and from appearances, impossible to tell it had ever been struck. Forcing his thoughts away from the accident, he merged onto the highway and headed for home. "I got that tray, so you'll be able t' talk to me once I get it setup in my bedroom. I hope you're right about no one being able to see the words but me."

Listening to the sound of the road, he chuckled to himself. Punching the button on the dash, music filled the small compartment. Tapping the wheel to the beat, he occupied himself the best he could for the few hours it would take to arrive in the small community where he grew up.

"There's my baby!" Bethany Phillips squealed when the tiny hybrid pulled up in the drive. Dashing out the door to greet him, the boy's father followed his wife into the warm Saturday morning air more calmly.

"Good t' see you, son," he called, grasping the boy's outstretched appendage and pulling him in for a clap on the back. "Been worried," he added more quietly.

"I know," Charlie nodded, "But I'm ok. It's been rough, but I think I'm gonna make it," the young man grinned. Turning to the back seat and the packed trunk space beyond, he wafted a hand. "I let the apartment go, an' brought all my stuff. Donna's mom took all o' her things, an' I figure I'll move back to the dorm if I go back next fall."

"If you go back!" his mother exclaimed, "What's that supposeda mean?"

Charlie ignored the question, instead opening a door and removing items. Clomping up the stairs with his final load a few minutes later, he acknowledged the frown that he wore solemnly; *you couldn't wait to get outta here, and didn' wanna come back.*

However, he had discovered having his dead girlfriend as his only companion had been difficult in every sense of the word. *I need to be home; at least for a while.* Opening the box he had placed on his desk, his eyes darted around in disgust; *why the hell did she move all my stuff?*

Taking in the new arrangement, he scowled at the bed that stood between the door and the left hand wall, pushed flush to the flat surface with the nightstand next to it. His dresser stood in the corner at the foot of it, and his desk had been positioned in the center of the right hand wall, which looked odd to him next to the closet door. With a small sigh, he shifted to the window and glared at his father mowing the yard below. *Mom an' I never have seen things eye to eye.*

Returning to his box, he pulled out a few items before turning his attention to a bag of purchases he had made that morning. Closing his door, he carried the baking sheet and canister of baby powder over to the dresser. Removing his mother's decorations and tossing them on the bed, he placed his tray on the flat surface, then sprinkled the white talc generously across it.

Clenching his jaw, he shook the pan gently from the edge, "Ok, baby; here we are."

Instantly, her invisible hand traced *hi* into the shallow coating, causing him to grin sheepishly.

"Ok, we're set then," he wafted a hand and cleared the letters. Unpacking the necessities, he stacked the unopened boxes into the bottom of the closet and ambled down the stairs. "Where's all my stuff?" he demanded when he entered the kitchen.

"What's of any value is in the storage building," his mother replied without facing him. "The rest I either tossed or donated…" her voice trailed away and she remained focused on the lunch she prepared.

Hearing the mower cut off outside, Charlie ambled out to join his father at the small shed behind their house. "Things still goin' good with you an' mom?"

"Sure are!" the older man grinned broadly while wiping his brow.

"Where's all my stuff?" he glanced around his father's workshop.

"Ah," John Phillips clamped him on the shoulder, "In the loft," he grabbed the stairs and pulled them down into position, "I know it probably seems a bit of a surprise, but you know how your mother is about the house."

"Yeah, I know," he mumbled before climbing the narrow flight of wobbly steps. Swinging his gaze over the stacks of boxes, he estimated only half of his old belongings remained. With a small sigh, he eased back down and closed the entrance; *I got the most important stuff when I left, anyways.*

"Mom's got lunch," he commented aloud, and the pair made their way inside so his father could wash up before the meal. Taking a seat at the kitchen table, Charlie inhaled deeply and allowed the air to escape with a soft sigh, resisting the temptation to throw a fit about having been erased from the household. *Mom does things how she wants, an' that's just the way it is.*

TWENTY-NINE

Out for Justice

FROM THE INVISIBLE plane of magical beings, Gous watched the trio in disgust, his eyes glowing a soft amber. Observing Charlie's shoulders hunched in a dejected manner, his lips twisted into a sneer; "Welcome home," he teased.

Scowling at the Dark Angel, Clarisse tossed her long blond strands, "You should leave," she clipped. "I'm back on this side, where I belong and you have no further business with him."

"Oh, but I do," he bared his pointed teeth as he hissed, "You have escaped the wrath of Keeper."

"As have you," she volleyed.

Gous emitted a low rumble of laughter, "Why do you resist, Summer Angel? There is no possible outcome here, other than the inevitable."

"Never," she gritted her teeth. "Be gone, Dark Angel."

His eyes dropped, taking in her tall frame, while their light grew brighter.

"Charlie, sit up straight!" Beth's voice interrupted the silence of their meal.

Swallowing his bite quickly, the young man removed the elbow he had been leaning on from the table, "Yes, ma'am."

"Stop it!" Clarisse moved to stand behind his chair.

"Make me," Gous taunted, taking a position behind the woman.

Looking down at the top of the brown head, the girl adjusted her shimmering locks, and a deep sadness settled over her. "Please, Gous. There are no winners here. None of us have gotten what we wanted. Go and let us be; I beg you."

"You beg of me?" his smile gave her an odd twist in her gut. "You think this is a game, with winners and losers?" The evil minion shook his head slowly, "No, my dear Clarisse; this is far deeper than any such trivial concerns."

Wiping angrily at an unexpected tear, her voice quavered, "How is it you were not destroyed?" she demanded. "Why is it you have returned after Keeper devoured you?"

"Oh, sweet angel," he breathed, "If you were mine, I might feel compelled to share what I know," he raised a hand as if to touch the woman of the house.

"Close your mouth when you chew," Beth demanded loudly while glaring at her son.

Fork suspended, Charlie stared at her, then cut his gaze over at his father, who watched the pair uneasily.

"Stop it!" Clarisse demanded, only receiving another laugh.

"I mean it, son," the woman pushed her chair back, "You act like you were raised in a barn, eatin' dinner like a pig at slop."

The two men exchanged a glance, and John reached for his glass. Missing his mark, the slippery container fell over out of his grasp, sending the liquid and ice rushing across the flat surface to cascade into his wife's lap.

Leaping to her feet, she sputtered and gasped. "Jesus Christ, John! Watch what the hell you're doin'!"

Charlie grimaced as the events unfolded, still holding his fork and curling his tongue. His mother grabbed a cup towel and wiped angrily at the mess. Casting his eyes about the room, his thoughts churned; *maybe Clarisse isn't the only one hanging around.* Scooping in a few more bites before dropping the remainder in the trash, he made a half-hearted apology, "Sorry, mom. I'll try to do better," and darted out the screen door.

Trotting down the drive, he made a left at the street and strutted along the worn path that ran parallel to the road. Not a large community, he had taken the route many times, and knew exactly where he was going. Arriving at the Dairy Queen a few minutes later, he paused with a hand resting on the door; *well, what are you waiting for?*

When Charlie had made his plans to leave the small east Texas town, he had hoped to never return. However, nothing in his life had worked out the way he wanted, especially the events that had followed his family's summer vacation a year ago. Mentally bracing himself, he pulled on the glass portal.

Inside, a cool blast of air hit him square in the face. Familiar scents and sounds engulfed him, and he paused to take in the small dining area, filled with six tables with chairs and a dozen booths that lined the walls. His eyes darted uncontrollably to the counter to his right, where a plump brunette ran the register and made ice cream sundaes.

Spying him when her line had cleared, Tabitha Turner emitted a loud squeal. Bouncing around the counter, she didn't bother to wait for his reaction, and grabbed him for a strong embrace.

THIRTY

Friends and Enemies

"EASY, TABS," Charlie worked his arms free and gave the girl a cursory pat on the back before extracting himself from her grasp.

Giggling, she stepped back, "Well, whadda you expect? You left without even sayin' goodbye last fall!"

The young man shook his head slowly, his hint of a smile easing the blow. Tabitha had been his best friend for many years, and for a time everyone had thought of the pair as a couple. Staring down into her deep brown eyes, he noted the new cut she sported, one that hardly qualified as feminine and did little to compliment her rounded form.

His mind drawn to his abrupt departure, he recalled that the young woman before him had never measured up to his expectations. Although they had been close ever since he could remember, he had been unable to consider her as more than a friend, even after their exploratory sexual encounters.

Tabitha on the other hand obviously adored him. Never having spoken an ill word to or about him, she had been heartbroken that he left her hanging. But then again, Charlie had always left her on the edge, only giving her cause to think there might be a chance, but never enough for it to be real.

"Well, well, look who decided to grace us with his presence!" a loud male voice interrupted their reunion, followed by a cascade of laughter from what seemed every corner of the room.

The DQ being one of only three suitable locations in town, it had been the hangout of the local teenagers for several decades. Casting his mahogany orbs around at the patrons, Charlie could see things hadn't changed much. Pulling himself further away from the clingy female, he clenched his jaw, "Hey, Brett, how's it hangin'?"

Brett Nelson laughed loudly, "How's it hangin'?" he mocked the younger male, "Whadda you care?"

Charlie's muscles in his neck rippled with his effort to remain civil, "Easy man. We ain't always got along, but that's no reason why we can't start over, right?"

"Sure, we can be pals," the freckle covered arm swung without warning, landing a blow to Charlie's upper left arm.

Knocked off balance, he caught himself while gripping the injured limb for a moment with a grimace. Recovering quickly, he adjusted his frame to stand at his full height. Matching the town bully toe to toe, he snarled, "Exactly. Le's let bygones be bygones," he offered his hand.

Giving him a shake, the redhead grinned broadly while squeezing the appendage more firmly than needed. After he had inflicted a sufficient show of force, he dropped the fingers and indicated a table, "Come on over. I'll buy you lunch!"

His toothy grin gave Charlie an uneasy feeling in his gut, and he briefly considered getting the hell out of there. But things at home were tenuous at best, and he would have to pick his poison. "I already ate," he huffed, choosing a chair while his eyes darted around at the rest of the group.

Taking his seat, he noted that almost everyone from the old days still remained; a group that he and Tabitha had never quite meshed with. Perhaps that's why he and the girl had formed a bond early on, and even though he had never thought of her as a love interest, he had to admit they were comrades in the truest sense of the word.

"Fine," Brett muttered, "Give 'im a Coke," he handed Tabitha a five-dollar bill, "An' get your fat ass back t' work!"

Charlie's eyes narrowed instantly as he took silent offense to the remark. Watching the girl's features deflate, he knew the pain she felt all too well; *nope, some things never change.*

Accepting the cup from her a few minutes later, he peeled the paper away from his straw and pointed it at the leader of the pack, "So, did you end up gettin' into college somewhere?"

"Naw, who needs that shit? I'm workin' for my ol' man over at the garage when he needs a hand," Brett grinned, exposing his crooked stains proudly. "Only a few o' you high an' mighty fuckers think you're too good for an honest day's work."

Charlie grinned, having been exposed to the attitude of the the Nelson clan his entire life. Brett's father owned and ran the gas station and quickie mart, as well as the Dairy Queen and the small grocery store. "Yeah, I guess you got it made, educated or not," he opened a palm towards his adversary, "But I'll find my place."

A wave of snickers followed, and Charlie looked around uneasily at Brett's cronies. *Man, just once I'd like to have the upper hand,* he lamented as he watched his nemesis pop a few ketchup laden fries into his mouth. *Wait a minute; I do have the upper hand.* A slow smile spread across his lips as he focused on the motion, and in the blink of an eye, the segment of potato had fallen and dotted Brett's white wife-beater with a bright red mark.

"Son of a bitch," he growled, wiping angrily at it with grease stained digits. Leaning forward to grab at the napkin dispenser, the back legs of his chair rose off of the floor.

With a flick of his wrist, Charlie gave the seat a mental shove, and Brett fell forwards, his chin smacking against the table on his way to the floor. Howling loudly, he caught the blood that dripped from his chin, and Charlie's brown eyes darted to the counter, where Tabitha laughed loudly at the spectacle, which only encouraged him to push for more.

"Wow, man, lemme give you a hand," he offered his injured target a fist full of paper towels to catch the red liquid that added to the bright stains on his shirt.

Brett accepted the wad and pressed them to his gushing lip, which he had bitten in the original fall. Clutching the edge of the table, he used it as support to get to his feet, when it suddenly toppled. Instead of standing, he found himself face down once more, with the flat surface landing on him and its contents spilling across his rear, marking the back side of his shirt and jeans with food and drinks.

Tabitha's laugh a loud cackle, a few of the others joined in, while Brett's pale skin shifted to a bright red beneath his plethora of beauty marks, "Son of a bitch! You guys shut the fuck up!"

Caught up in the moment, Charlie chuckled as he continued to covertly use his newfound powers to settle the score. For years, the man before him had badgered and bullied those he did not like. Being a year or two older and always bigger, he had used his talents and position to give nothing but pain to any he did not deem worthy of breathing his air, and Charlie could see that perhaps some things had changed after all.

The floor coated in the remnants of his meal, Brett hit the hard flat surface every time he tried to stand, pushed by an invisible force determined to keep him down.

Sharing brief eye-contact with the young woman, Charlie's smile faded slightly, and a stab of guilt penetrated his mood. Reaching down, he clamped the older boy on the shoulder and hauled him to his feet.

"Wow, Brett; I never knew you was a clumsy oaf," he chortled.

"I said shut the fuck up," his victim's thin lips snarled as he shoved his aid away.

"No problem, man," Charlie showed his palms while taking a step back, and laughing loudly, "Hey, I gotta go. It was real good seeing you again!" Turning his back on the scene, he slapped the counter, "You wanna meet up later, Tabs?"

Grinning ear to ear, the girl nodded. "Sure, Charlie! I get off at five, if you wanna pick me up, say six or six-thirty?" Still Charlie's fool, all he had to do was ask.

"Sounds great, I'll get you at six then, at your parents' place?"

"Yup; home sweet home!"

"All right," he called over his shoulder and headed for the door, leaving the group that surrounded his arch-enemy in his wake.

THIRTY-ONE

Date Night

CHARLIE PULLED up in front of the Turner residence at six pm on the dot. Casting a quick glance at the back seat filled with his surprise, he grinned and opened the door. Picking his way through the weeds in the front yard to the porch, Tabitha bounded out the front, heading him off before he could knock.

"Dad's passed out on the couch," she warned, catching his arm and guiding him away.

"Already?"

"Yeah," she glanced nervously over her shoulder while he opened the door for her.

Taking her over-sized purse, he chuckled, "Here, lemme put this in the back for you." Dropping it onto his blanket, he made his way around and slid behind the wheel, catching the scent of perfume that filled the cramped space. Lowering the window, he remembered it had been his favorite, "So, what's up with your ol' man?"

"Uh, well," she adjusted herself nervously, "Things aren't good."

Picking up on her tension, he reached for her hand, "Come on, I'm your oldest friend. You can tell me."

"He lost his job," she admitted quietly. "Got fired, actually, an' mom took off with some other guy."

Stunned, Charlie squeezed her firmly, "Wow!" Unable to form a coherent reply for a moment, he focused on his driving, making the cut off that led to a secluded spot outside of town; their spot.

"Are we visiting the boonies?" she grinned at the familiar path.

"We sure are!" his voice bright, he nodded vigorously. "I really am sorry t' hear about your folks, Tabs. I know that's rough."

"It's ok," she sniffed slightly, "He deserved t' get left. If I had anywhere to go, I'd leave myself."

"He's not hitting you, is he?"

"No," she defended quickly; almost too quickly. "He's a drunk, Charlie. He has a beer for breakfast, liquor for lunch, and sleeps it off for dinner."

"Yeah," he pulled his hand away to grasp the wheel firmly as the trail diminished. "Looks like no one's been out here in a while."

"Naw, I ain't been out here since before you left, an' not too many know about this place." She emitted a small sigh when they passed the last set of trees and pulled into the clearing; an area open to the sky that measured about thirty by thirty feet square.

Climbing out, Charlie cast his gaze around at the mixed lot of trees that formed the small circle. "I brought a picnic," he commented casually, "You wanna grab the blanket an' I'll get the fire set up?"

"A fire!" she exclaimed, "I think we better pass on that. Things have been pretty dry around here this year."

"Oh," he laughed, hoisting his large basket of food and placing it on the hood. "All right, no fire. You want a Coke?" he inquired casually, opening the doors wide and setting the radio's volume.

"Sure," she knelt down on her fresh spread and smiled at the floral print.

"Ok, one sec," he rummaged in the ice chest after placing it at the front of the car on the ground.

"I've really missed you, Charlie," she commented while accepting the frosty can.

Not bothering to reply, he felt a stab of guilt as he pulled out their plates. Handing her one and placing his on the pristine covering, he located the linen napkins and a canister of wet wipes. Dropping onto the blanket next to her, he smiled nervously, causing her to giggle.

"What's the matter, baby? Have things really changed that much between us?" she pulled at her roasted chicken and began to nibble.

"It's been a while," he admitted quietly.

"Yeah, I know," she watched him with tender brown eyes. "I was sorry t' hear about your girlfriend. Really, I was. I wanted you t' be happy, baby, even if it wadn' with me."

Charlie nodded, tearing into his own dinner. A knot forming in the pit of his stomach, he did his best to devour the meal, and the couple ate in a peaceful quiet. Watching the sun disappear behind the tall stand of trees, he wiped his fingers on his rag and gathered his dishes. "So, you're not seeing anyone?" he finally broke the silence.

"Nope," she clipped, gathering her own items and standing to place them in the box.

"Ah," he grinned, having already guessed that. Watching her fumble around in her bag, he gasped at her surprise, "Where the hell did you get those?"

"Whadda ya mean?" she grinned, handing him one of the bottles, "I tol' you, my ol' man's a drunk. There's liquor all over the place at home."

Staring at the golden liquid, he sighed loudly, "I guess so. But I have t' tell you something. I really loved Donna; an' I don't think I should have come here with you."

"It's ok," she smiled down at her own container, opening it and adding a generous amount to one of the cups of ice she had filled, "You want Jack or Rum?"

"I don't know about this," he pushed. "I think that I'm using you, an' I don't like how that feels."

"It's ok, Charlie," she poured the fizzy soda in with the mixture. "I want you to feel better. I wanna take care o' you, an' if this is what it takes... then so be it."

He nodded, giving her a small chuckle. Lifting his own cup, he reached for the bottle she had used as well, "I'll take this; I don't like Jack. Unless I'm wasted, an' then he's not so bad."

Sipping on the drinks, the pair sat on the blanket and faced one another while he opened up about how things had been at school. Unable to tell her about the most recent developments, or the circumstances behind his girlfriend's death, he kept it simple and hoped she understood.

Pouring their third glasses for them, Tabitha filled his three-quarters with the Jack and topped it off with a splash of soda. "Here you go, sir," she handed him the fresh drink and sat down next to him this time, placing her hand on his shoulder for a squeeze. When he didn't pull away, she continued to fondle him, massaging his arm and back.

Gulping the concoction, Charlie continued to wrestle with the idea of what would come next. They had been each other's firsts, years ago in fact; *when we were in junior high an' didn't know any better.* Since then, he had come to realize his feelings for her were not the foundation of a lasting relationship, and he had put an end to their visits to the place they currently shared. *What are you doing here?* he demanded to himself.

Gulping the last of his beverage, he tossed the ice into the grass and announced, "I'm done."

"Not yet, you're not," she breathed in his ear, having manipulated her way next to him to physically probe his manly frame. "You've grown up a lot since I had you last," she sighed.

"Yeah; I guess that I have," he tried to extricate himself from her grasp. "Tabs, listen. I really think this's a bad idea," his mind leapt to the tall blonde he felt certain would be watching them.

Pushing against his chest, the girl lay over the top of him, pressing her lips to his. Charlie only half-heartedly resisted, as the liquor had removed a hefty portion of his resolve. A few minutes later, he began to remove her clothing, and his fingers found their way across her soft folds of flesh around her waist.

Rolling her over, he placed her beneath him. "Let me handle this," he slurred, "You jus' look at the stars," he tried to appear suave. His fingers fumbling with his belt, his need pushed him to act.

"I don' see any stars," she mumbled.

Pausing, he sat back on his haunches and stared up at the sky above them. There were no twinkling lights visible, as dark clouds had rolled in to cover them, and a stiff wind blew against him. The edge of the blanket caught in the gust, Charlie grabbed it and forced it back down; *shit!*

An instant later, a torrent of rain pelted the couple. A flash of lightning lit up Tabitha's features, and he could see the fear in her eyes at the sudden storm. "Grab the stuff!" he commanded, already on his feet and headed to the trunk with the ice chest. Soaked to the bone a few minutes later, the couple managed to ease the vehicle out of the secluded spot and headed for home.

THIRTY-TWO

Call of the Angels

STUMBLING up the stairs to his room, Charlie felt in awe that he had managed to drop the girl at her house and make it home in one piece. Gripping the banister, he could tell he made too much noise, but in his inebriated state, he felt powerless to prevent it. Closing his door loudly, he wanted to scream.

"Where the hell are you?" he blurted loudly, making his way to the chest of drawers and slamming his fist down next to the pan of powder. "I know you did this, Clarisse!" Staring at the fine substance, nothing moved.

"Answer me, God dammit!" he ran his fingers through his brown waves, then worked to free them as they became caught in the tangles.

Do you love her? the words finally appeared.

Charlie glared at the message, fighting to control his anger. Pursing his lips, he sputtered, "It don't matter, that's not the point. You're dead, Clarisse! You have no right t' meddle in my life!" When the message remained unchanged, he pushed on, "I want you t' leave. You hear me? I don' think you followin' me around is a good idea anymore."

Kicking off his shoes, the young man fell across the bed and lost consciousness. Clarisse stared down at his tall frame, tears dripping unchecked onto her white silk blouse. Turning to the tray, she cleared the message and dragged her finger through the soft material once more.

"Where are you off to?" Gous interrupted her thoughts.

"I don't know," she returned dejectedly. "He doesn't want to be helped, and I can't force him."

The Dark Angel grinned, "Leaving him to me then, are you? I like this. Join me, Clarisse. What else is there for you to do?"

Blinking at the bed for a moment, she realized she had missed her old duties. *And Charlie doesn't want me here.* "It's none of your concern," she sniffed, before she disappeared.

Charlie awoke some time later, the remnants of alcohol still coursing through his veins. Driven by the need to urinate, he opened his door and stumbled down the hall. Arriving in his bathroom, he closed the door and flicked on the light, then shut it off while squinting his eyes heavily.

Leaning over the sink, he relieved himself, not daring to try and hit the toilet. Then running the cold water, he rinsed the bowl and used it to wash his face; *well, that was a fiasco.* Drying himself roughly, he made his way back to his room and switched on the small lamp that sat on his desk before he shuffled over to his pan.

"I'm sorry, baby," he leaned his head into his palms and stared at her final words. "I didn't mean it," he sighed.

"It's too late," Gous sang into the air next to him, mocking the man who couldn't hear him. "She has left you to me, and oh, what fun we are going to have!"

Tears stung his eyes as Charlie removed his clothing and slid between the sheets. Everything in his life had been chaos for so long. *Jesus Christ, why can't I just be normal?*

When he awoke again, bright sunlight filled his room. Laying his hands over his face to block it, he retraced the dream that had occurred only a few minutes before. *Keeper,* he breathed. *That's his name.* He recalled the fight that he had shared with some dark creature as well. He still only knew bits and pieces of what had taken place while he was dead, but the parts he did know were enough to strike fear into the depths of his being.

"I'm sorry, Clarisse," he spoke aloud, not expecting a reply. Rising, he gathered fresh clothes and made his way to the shower. Arriving in the kitchen a few minutes later, he discovered his mother cleaning away, as if the world spun in perfect harmony around them.

"Anything for breakfast?" he inquired.

"It's in the fridge," she avoided looking at him, jumping slightly when the phone on the wall rang. The house phone had been kept for emergencies, and few had the number. To have it interrupt them, probably a salesman, annoyed her greatly. Grabbing the receiver, "Hello!" she said forcefully.

A moment later, the color drained from her features, and Charlie heard the sound of the device hitting the floor at the same instant that a low wail filled the room. Turning to face her, he could see the panic in her eyes, and demanded, "Mom, what's wrong?"

"It's John," she gasped, dropping to her knees to retrieve the earpiece and return it to its cradle, "He's at the hospital. We have to go, right now!"

Gathering her purse, Charlie found his keys and led her out to his car, "I'll drive." With her in the passenger seat, he skillfully maneuvered the vehicle to the only medical facility in the small town.

Inside, a nurse met them in front of the counter, and requested that Charlie remain outside while his mother followed the young female to the back. With an exasperated breath, his gaze swung around the small area, taking in the collection of people waiting for news on their loved ones. All the seats were taken, so he located a small section of wall on the far side and leaned against it anxiously.

A short time later, he became aware of a hooded figure standing next to him. Not wanting to stare, he studied the man for several minutes before realizing that it was not a brown hoodie that he wore. Instead, the tall male stood cloaked in a long brown robe. Glaring at him straight on, he could feel the tingle work it's way up his spine; *oh my God, this cannot be happening!*

"You know, you look like the grim reaper," he whispered loudly, a small smirk teasing his lips. Several of the other occupants heard his observation and stared at him. "Are you here for my dad?" he said a little more loudly.

"Mommy, why is that man talking to himself?" a young girl seated across from him asked.

"I have no idea, baby," the woman replied, her eyes cut up at him warily.

Taken aback, his gaze darted back towards the man he guessed to be Keeper. With a start, he gasped, "Where the hell did he go?"

Grasping the girl next to her, the woman asked quietly, "Are you high?"

Charlie blinked at her for several seconds, too stunned to reply. "No," he finally managed, using his palms to rub his eyes heavily, "I'm tired, I guess." Crossing the room with crisp steps, he inquired at the desk, "Nurse; is there anything you can tell me about my father?"

"Not at this time," she didn't even look at him. "We'll call you when we know anything."

"Great," he muttered and headed out the front door. Outside, the air had warmed considerably, and a hot Texas sun shown down brightly. Walking past the small collection of smokers huddled around a large ashtray, he found a strip of sidewalk away from everyone else, and called quietly, "Clarisse? Baby, please tell me you really didn't leave."

"She left," a deep male voice replied.

Swinging around with a grunt, Charlie gaped at the tall figure, whose skin appeared a deep bronze. His hand trembling, he reached out to touch the dark brown robe, his heart pounding wildly in his chest as his fingers seemed to pass through the course material; *holy shit!* "Who the fuck're you?"

"You know who I am, son," the greatest of all angels breathed, "I know you remember me."

Nodding slightly, his Adam's apple moved up and down as he swallowed, "Ok, yeah, I guess I recall a little bit. What're you doin' here? What do you want from me?"

"Walk with me," Keeper replied, and the young man obediently fell into step beside him. "I've been watching you for a long time, Charlie. And don't worry, no one else can see me," he wafted a hand to indicate the cars that passed on the busy street.

"So how come I can see you?" Charlie gasped, his shock evident. "I thought there was some plane business that kept you guys on the other side. I don't know; some magic shit."

Keeper's laughter rumbled as he turned to the young man, stopping at the corner, "You are so very special, Charlie. You do not yet know for what purpose you have been raised, but I assure you, the time is very close. With every task you have been given, you have proven to be exceptional."

"Task?" Charlie shoved his hands into his front pockets, "You mean you've been testing me?"

"Something like that," the ancient angel smiled lopsidedly. "All great men face trials and tribulations, my child. For that is what makes them great."

"I see," he grimaced, "So have I passed your little test, then?"

"No," Keeper raised his hand, indicating the tall building to his right, "Your greatest challenge yet awaits you," and in an instant, he vanished.

"Oh, no!" Charlie gasped, staring up at the glass windows glistening in the bright light. Running full speed to the entrance, he pounded his fist onto the counter, "I need to see my father, right now!"

At that moment, a set of double doors leading to the back parted, and his mother exited the wide frame. She carried herself stiffly, her progress slow and deliberate. When she reached him, he could tell she had been crying, as her swollen red eyes evidenced the fact clearly.

"What's happened?" he breathed, his hands grasping her arms and sliding up to squeeze them just below her shoulders.

"Your dad," she began, her breath moving in and out of her wide open mouth with great effort. "He's gone, Charlie. He had a heart attack, an' he left us." Her voice ended with a loud sob, and she collapsed limply against him.

THIRTY-THREE

Keeper's Minion

CHARLIE STARED at the dark flecks, stirring them slowly with the straw and causing them to swirl through the light pink mixture. He had buried his father that morning, and had walked to the Dairy Queen out of lack for anything better to do.

"How's the shake?" Tabitha asked as she sank down onto the leather covered seat across from him.

"It's fine," he muttered. "You know, I've lost two people in six weeks. Are you sure you wanna hang out with me?"

"Why?" she giggled, "You think you're cursed or something? Is the boogie man gonna get me?"

"Maybe," his mind darted to Keeper and his dark minion. "Have you ever felt like someone was really out to get you?"

"No," she sighed, reaching to clasp his hand lightly between hers, "No, baby; no one is out to get you. It's bad luck, that's all. You're in a rough spot right now, an' you need your friends to help you through it."

His face still glaring at the cup, he cut his eyes up at her, "You have no idea what's out there," he growled.

Startled by his altered demeanor, she slowly withdrew her trembling digits, "I guess I don't. You've been really different since you got back."

Lifting his chin, he roughly ran his fingers across his mouth and face.

Exhaling loudly, he nodded, "Yeah. I'm not who I used to be," and chuckled at the familiarity of the idea. "I have to go," he stood abruptly, leaving her staring after him as he pushed on the glass door and sauntered down the road.

Making his way along the path, his mind turned. *My greatest challenge,* he repeated for the umpteenth time. *What if I refuse your damn challenge?* All he wanted at that moment was to have Clarisse back. *Even if I have to talk to her across a pan filled with talc.*

He knew he had to find her, one way or another. *But where do I look?* Inside the house, he quietly took to the stairs. He wanted to make his getaway fast and clean; *no use alerting mom that I'm taking off.*

At the door to his room, he stopped cold. On the far side, his mother stood next to his chest of drawers, peering down into his baking sheet. "What're you doing?" he demanded crossly.

"Oh!" she looked up with a jolt, "I'm sorry, Charlie. I was just in here... thinking." She glanced at the container, "And I saw this. Kinda odd, ya know?" She wafted her hand at it, "What's it for?"

His anger boiled over, "It's none o' your business, that's what it's for!"

Her jaw dropped at his display, "Jesus, son, calm down! It was a simple question, an' no reason t' get all huffy!"

His eyes flicked to the flat surface, the words *Goodbye Charlie* remaining clearly visible, and he recalled that other people wouldn't be able to see them. *At least, Clarisse said they can't. Only the chosen can see;* that was the first rule. "It's powder, mom," he stated in a calmer tone and waited.

"Ok," she shrugged, "I'll respect your privacy." She made her way to the door, closing it behind her.

Alone in the room, the young man moved quickly, tossing a few changes of clothes into one of his bags. Dumping the tray into the trash, he shoved it into the pack as well, along with the container of powder. *This is insane,* he coughed at the cloud that hung in the air. *But I have to try.*

Gliding quietly down the stairs, he hoped to avoid seeing his mother, and thereby making it into his car in peace. However, she had seen him slinking along and had caught up with him as he tossed the pack into the trunk, and inquired sharply, "Where do you think you're going?"

"Mom!" he screamed with a jump. Turning to face her, his pulse pounded in his ears, "I'm gonna get away for a few days."

"Away?" she stared incredulously. "I just lost your father, an' you're leavin' me alone?"

Curling his tongue nervously, Charlie tried to think of a good explanation. Coming up empty, he tried for something closer to the truth. "I need to get away for a few days; that's all."

"An' where are you going?" her tone dripped with resentment.

"I don't really know," he admitted. "I have the sudden urge to drive. Maybe go see the ocean or somethin'."

"You're goin' t' Corpus?" her eyebrows shot up.

"Not that ocean," he squirmed. "I'm thinkin' California… for a few days. I'll be back in a week or two, I promise." Sliding around to the front, he opened the driver's side and climbed in. To his amazement, she slid into the passenger side and closed the door behind her. "What the hell are you doing?" he glared at her profile.

"I'm not stayin' here alone," she stared at the glass in front of her.

"You can't up an' leave!"

"Why not? Your dad was my whole world, remember? I don' work, an' suddenly, I got nothin' to do but take care of an empty house…" her voice trailed away and he could see her bottom lip had begun to quiver.

"Aww, mom, stop that, ok?"

Sniffing loudly, she bellowed, "Why is it you never cared about me? Not ever, since you was little!"

"What the hell do you mean I never cared about you?" he replied tartly, "Look, jus' get out. I'm not gonna sit here an' fight with you over whether or not I love my momma. I got better things t' do."

Reaching over her shoulder, she grabbed the seat belt and fastened it with a sharp click. Wiping at her tear coated cheeks, she spit through clenched teeth, "You ain't leavin' me here, an' that's final." She still hadn't looked at him, and he really couldn't tell how far she was willing to take it.

"So we're gonna drive off an' leave the house standin' wide open?"

Bethany didn't reply. Instead, she focused on her breathing and tried to calm her trembling limbs.

"Fine!" his voice rose, "I'll lock the fucking door, but you don' even have a change o' clothes!"

The woman still didn't respond, so he hauled his tall frame out of the seat, slamming his door and causing the tiny car to shake in the process. Stomping up the front steps, he climbed the stairs while he fumed; *fucking bitch. She pulls this tug-of-war shit way too often, an' I'm sick of it.* Making it to the master bedroom, a wave of sadness hit him at the sight of his father's things still neatly arranged on his dresser.

Swallowing hard, he forced himself to move about the room, gathering a few changes of clothes for her. Deciding to grab a spare pair of shoes as well, he placed them all in a suitcase from out of the closet. *I wonder if Gous killed him,* he contemplated as he descended into the entryway. It was a heavy blow, either way.

Locking the front door, he placed her bag into the trunk next to his own, and slid behind the wheel. "I got you some clothes," he confessed. "Do you need anything else? Medicine or anything?"

"No," she replied more calmly.

"All right, then let's get one thing straight. You wanted to come with me, but this is *my* trip. We will go where I wanna go, an' stop where I wanna stop. You got me?"

His mother nodded, her lips pursing as a fresh wave of tears welled in her eyes.

"Jesus," he muttered, pulling a paper napkin out of his cubby in the door, "Here," he waved it at her and then started the car. Rolling out onto the road, he made for the highway, while wishing like hell he had gotten away without her.

THIRTY-FOUR

Unraveled

CHARLIE GUIDED the tiny hybrid into the covered driveway in front of the hotel. Cutting off the switch, he heaved a small sigh, "You coming in?"

"I'll wait," she sniffed.

Opening the door, he grabbed the frame and used it to extricate himself from the cramped space while muttering, "Car's too damn small for traveling."

Inside, he made his request and presented the young man with his father's credit card. It had been given to him for emergencies when he left for college, and although he had not mentioned to his mother that he used it to pay for their little holiday, he didn't really care what she would think about it if she knew.

Accepting the plastic a few minutes later, he signed the page, and picked up the key-card, "Thanks, man."

Back out front, he parked the car and the pair gathered their luggage. They had been together about thirty hours, and spent one night in a hotel already. *And we've said maybe ten words to one another,* he lamented. His mother could be pretty stubborn, he had to give her that.

Inside their quarters, Charlie chose the bed closest to the window and stated matter-of-factly, "I'm getting a shower. We can order room service tonight." Not waiting for a reply, he stepped into the lavatory and kicked on the warm cascade.

Half an hour later, he applied the towel briskly to his brown shocks of hair, then dropped the cloth to listen more closely. Hearing what sounded like his mother arguing with someone, he grabbed the door and wrenched it open, demanding, "What's going on out here?"

Placing her hand over the mouthpiece, the woman snapped, "They don't wanna serve us," and returning it to her ear, she continued, "I don't care what time it is or what time the kitchen closes. We are guests in your hotel, an' we wanna be fed!"

"Oh, my God," Charlie muttered in irritation, dropping the towel on the floor and reaching for his bag, "Forget it mom! Hang up an' I'll take you t' get somethin' to eat."

Doing as he instructed, Beth moved to the bathroom to take care of her own needs while he dressed. Coming out a few minutes later, she followed him down to his car.

Leaning on his palm, elbow pressed against the glass, Charlie sighed loudly, "What do you want?"

"I don't care, pick a place."

Swinging into the next parking lot, he announced, "This looks good," while she gave the small structure a dubious glare. Not waiting for her comment, he got out and headed inside.

A few minutes later, they had ordered steaks with baked potatoes and salad. Staring at her dark features, he thought about how much he looked like her, rather than his father. "I'm sorry I got all mad you wanted to come," he shrugged slightly as he apologized. "I didn't understand why you would want to."

Smiling slightly, she reached over to pat the back of his hand, "It's ok, son. I forgive you."

"You forgive me," he repeated, running a hand around his tired neck, "Wow, that's swell."

"What?" she appeared surprised.

Chuckling, he shook his head, "We never have gotten along. Not ever that I can think of. Why is that?"

"I dunno," she showed him her palms, "I guess I've never really felt connected to you."

"Not connected to me," he repeated, "Why is that? Am I adopted an' you never told me?"

"No," she laughed loudly, "You weren't adopted, baby. I jus' had a hard time when you were born, with the labor an' everything, an' even the pregnancy before that. After you got here, it seemed t' carry over, like you were a stranger t' me."

Charlie sighed, tapping the table with his fingers, "We don't really have anything in common, do we."

"I dunno," she confessed, "I'm your mom; I think that makes us pretty connected, even if it's hard for me."

He laughed at the observation, "Yeah, well, I guess it does." Waiting until their meal had been served and she had begun to eat, he then continued, "So what are you going to do now that dad's gone?"

"I don' really know," she shook her long brown hair, "I guess I'll need to get a job an' stay busy. I'm sure you'll go back t' school, either in Austin, or some place else."

"Yeah," he agreed quickly, "I've been thinking that I need t' go back an' finish. I need t' get a good job so I can look after you as you get older."

Her face instantly turned to stone, "What's that supposed t' mean?"

Charlie stared at her, his mouth hanging open slightly, "It means I need to be able to provide for you if I need to, since dad's gone. Jesus Christ, woman, why is everything I say an' do ALWAYS a problem with you?"

Bethany glared at him, the anger in her gut churning, "Because you always are! Always into stuff, making a mess after I worked all day to clean things! Playing games an' horsin' around rather than helping! Oh, but your dad is gone so *now* you wanna make yourself useful!"

Charlie held his arms out wide, staring at her in disbelief, "You mean to tell me you're still pissed at me about things I did... when I was a kid?"

"Shut up, Charlie!" she clipped, returning to her meal and shoving bites in her mouth as quickly as she could.

This isn't rational, he glared at the top of her head as she bent over her plate. Feeling as if the air had come on above him, he shivered slightly, casting his gaze around the room. Not seeing anything of importance, he returned to his own dinner, and greedily polished off the plate.

Taking the woman back to the hotel when they were done, he contemplated where he might set up his powder pan. When she moved to take her own shower, he pulled it out and placed it on the table next to the window and stared at it for a long moment. *Fuck it,* he finally breathed, and sprinkled a thin layer of the diaper treatment across it.

Taking a seat in one of the cushioned chairs, he still sat staring at it when the bathroom door opened, and a small puff of steam followed her into the room. "What're you doing?" she demanded when she noticed his transfixed state.

Only flicking a brief glance in her direction, he countered, "You wouldn't believe me if I told you."

Watching as he shifted uncomfortably in the chair and adjusted his feet beneath the table, she moved closer, "Try me."

"No," he shook his head, "I'm not allowed to discuss it..." his voice trailed away at the brief idea that he technically wasn't an angel, and their rules didn't apply to him. Cutting his eyes over at her stoic features, he grunted, "Ok, I'm talking to Clarisse."

"Clarisse," she repeated, dumbfounded. "And Clarisse... bakes inedible cookies?"

Charlie laughed out loud at her confused expression, her repetition of the name bringing him up short, "Sorry. Donna," he clarified.

Intrigued, she stepped forward and rested her hands on the back of the chair facing him. "Ok, why is Donna now Clarisse, an' how are you talkin' to her?"

He could hear the concern in her voice, and realized she still cared about him, even though they had always seemed at odds, "I'm ok, mom. I'm not crazy." Glancing hurriedly around the small space, he grinned, "Siddown, an' I'll tell you about it."

Sliding timidly into the seat, Beth kept her eyes on her son's face. Panic had gripped her the moment he had spoken, as flashbacks from his childhood had bombarded her.

"Clarisse is what Donna told me her real name was. She told me she was an angel and that -"

"Stop it, Charlie!" his mother cut him off. "No more angel talk!"

Frowning, he made a popping noise with his lips, "No more, huh? Have we talked about angels before?"

"When you were little," she flinched, "I thought you had outgrown that."

"Ohhh," he leaned back in the chair, "I see. You remember about Charlie's Angel."

"She isn't real, son," Beth gritted her teeth.

"Umm," he gave her a crooked grin. "Then there's nothing else to say."

"What's the pan for, son?"

"I told you, it's for talking to Clarisse," he chuckled, "Only you don't wanna hear it. An' she's not answering anyways." He looked down at his hands as he shrugged. "I kinda pissed her off, an' she left. An' I think there's a Dark Angel hanging around an' messing with us. I think that's why you're always pissed off at me."

"A Dark Angel," she sighed, fearing that her son was in worse shape than she had thought. "Baby, how long is this gonna go on?"

Charlie burst into laughter, his mind drawn to the few short weeks ago when Clarisse had revealed herself to him. "Watch this, mom," he raised his hand and traced a few letters into the fine coating. "You see that?"

"Yes, I see it."

Rising from the chair, he moved around behind it and placed his back against the wall. With a wave of his hand, he used his power to remove the message, then waited for her response. When she sat blinking, her expression unchanged, he demanded, "Well?"

"Well, what?"

"Well, what do you think?" he stepped forward and wafted a hand over the pristine grains.

"It says *Charlie*," she replied calmly, "What is it you're tryin' to do?"

His jaw dropped, he glared at her, "You still see my name?"

"Of course I do, what did you expect me to see?"

Covering his mouth with trembling fingers, his mind raced. "Nothing, mom. I didn't expect you to see anything. I'm ok, an' we need to get some sleep." Turning to the bed, he pulled back the blankets and slid between the sheets. *What if everything that happened with Donna was in my head?* He lay still and blinked at the ceiling; *what if my magic isn't real, and my mind is coming unraveled?* What does a person do when they think they may have gone crazy?

THIRTY-FIVE

Laid to Rest

LEAVING New Mexico behind them the following day, Bethany watched her son through hollow eyes. She had hardly slept the previous night, and fear had her firmly in its grasp. They had never been close, and she realized that much of that had been her doing, but they needed each other at this moment, in a way that they never had before.

Pulling up at a diner on the outskirts of Phoenix in the smaller town of Casa Grande, she followed the young man inside for an early dinner. Choosing seats at a table in the center of the floor, she smiled at him, "This's a nice place."

Charlie froze, "Really," aware that compliments were not her thing. Shifting into the chair across from her, he nodded, "I guess you're still freaked out about last night."

"No," she countered quickly, "I'm ok. Consider that whole incident... laid to rest."

"Ah," he gave her a knowing grin, "So if we ignore it, it'll go away, is that it?"

Her eyes darted nervously around them, and her voice grew quieter, "I know you've been under a lot of stress, baby. First Donna, an' then your daddy. You need a chance to rest, an' get yourself together." Interrupted by the waitress, she gave the elderly lady her order.

Watching the wrinkled hands as they scribbled on her pad, Charlie thought of Grandma Parker. *It had to be real.* He could not simply have imagined all that took place. Giving her his order as well, he smiled up at her warm green eyes. *I need a way to show mom that I'm not losing my mind.*

Of course the whole *chosen* business would be tricky, as she had clearly not fallen into that category. *And Clarisse said I could get into trouble for revealing the other plane.* His thoughts continued to churn while they ate.

"Excuse me," a man stopped at their table and planted himself in an empty chair. "Pardon the interruption, but would you be headed to California?"

"Why, yes," Beth blurted before Charlie interrupted her.

"No, actually we're not," he clarified, giving his mother an unwavering stare.

Stunned, she blinked at him rapidly, "Have you changed your mind? I thought you wanted to see the ocean."

"Yeah, I did," he stammered, cutting his glare over at the gentleman, noting that he appeared clean shaven and not your typical drifter. "Sorry, man."

"Sorry for what?" the interloper's blue eyes glared at him coolly, "I simply asked if you were headed that way. I actually did not indicate why."

Charlie's jaw dropped, realizing that he had jumped the gun. "Ok, we're going to California."

"Good," a grin slowly stretched across his handsome features, and he reached for Beth's hand to wrap it between his. "I need a ride."

Charlie slapped the table with an open palm, "Now, wait a minute!"

"It's quite all right, baby," his mother cut him off, her mood oddly jovial, "There's plenty o' room, an' I think we would enjoy the company."

Glaring at her, the younger man shook his head slowly, "You can't be serious. We don't even know this guy!"

"Ah, Phillip Parson," he offered him a hand, "Please, call me Phil."

Refusing to shake the appendage, Charlie stood and stormed up to the counter, ready to pay out. *No fucking way this is a coincidence,* he fumed. *Some guy shows up, asking for a ride.* Gous was up to something, he knew it. *Please, Clarisse, where the hell are you?*

Climbing into the car a short time later, Charlie scowled at the smile his mother wore as she slid into the back seat behind their passenger. Taking the front, Phil calmly adjusted the seat to allow for his long legs and snapped his restraint into place.

Passing through Phoenix and its sprawling suburbs, Charlie kept his thoughts on his driving. At the same time, his mother chattered happily with the hitchhiker, plying him with questions about his origins, employment, and family, as well as sharing much of her own, as if they were old friends. Once they had come out the other side of the interstate, the traffic lessened as the sun began to set, and the young man felt safe to join the conversation.

Cutting his eyes over for quick covert glances, he noted that the man wore dark blue denim jeans and a button down shirt with short sleeves. Both articles appeared clean and pressed, and his haircut trimmed and neat. "So, Phil," he interrupted, "What's got you stranded in the middle of the desert?"

The soft blue eyes stared at him as the older man appeared in no hurry to divulge that particular piece of information. Instead, he adjusted himself more squarely into the seat and called to the woman behind him, "It was very nice to meet you, Beth."

"Oh, likewise," she agreed. Stretching behind him, she emitted an exaggerated yawn, "Well, it looks like we won' be stoppin' for a bit, an' I'm exhausted."

"I'm afraid not," Charlie admitted quietly, "Catch a nap, mom. I'll wake you in an hour or two," he suggested while flicking on the headlights.

Leaning her arm against the window, she breathed noisily, and soon fell asleep in the awkward silence that followed her son's unwelcome interrogation. Stealing glances at her in the rearview mirror, Charlie's features drew into a heavy frown as she disappeared into the darkness.

"You should be careful what you tell her," Phil stated bluntly, his eyes still watching the terrain through the window to his right.

His jaw dropped, Charlie shifted anxiously, "What's that supposed t' mean?"

"It means, I know who you are."

Swallowing the lump in his throat, the younger man worked to calm his panic, "Ok, let's assume for a minute that you do. Perhaps you'll tell me how you came by that knowledge?"

Phil's white teeth glinted in the shadows as he laughed, "Come on Charlie, surely you didn't think you were the only one?" A brief silence followed as the question hung in the air between them.

"No, I didn't think I was the only one," he finally admitted, "But I didn't think there would be any way t' recognize each other, either."

"Oh, there are ways," his passenger chuckled.

"So how did you end up stranded where we just happened to be? Or did someone send you to meet us?"

"I left my car at the cafe. Don't worry, I'll catch a ride back that way once I'm finished with you," his voice dropped slightly as he spoke. "I guess you could say that I was sent, but that's not exactly how it works."

"Really," Charlie sighed, "I wouldn't know how it works. I hardly know anything, an' what I do know scares the shit outta me."

"That'll pass. And you'll get used to being different."

"So you were rifted?" Charlie's tone had become even, fear and anger giving way to curiosity.

"Yes, I have seen the other side," the dark haired gentleman admitted. "And I have my gifts that I carry with me."

"I see; so you can manipulate objects as well. Tell me something, why do the angels look after us? What difference do we make to them?" As soon as he spoke, he could hear the laughter from the other side of the car. "Is that funny?"

"What makes you think we matter to them?"

"I dunno," he shrugged, "They look out for us."

"No, they look out for themselves," Phil corrected, cutting his eyes over at the boy, "What they may or may not do for us is a means to an end. We are like pets to them; cats and dogs."

Charlie pursed his lips, "You sound pretty cynical."

"I guess I am. You know what makes people happy?" he only paused for an instant, and then ploughed on, "People are happy because they don't know. That's why you shouldn't poison your mother's life. Don't burden her with things she wasn't meant to understand."

"But that's cruel, don't you think? To know and *not* share?"

The silence between them grew thick. After a long pause, Phillip admitted, "Charlie, I know what you're going through. I was fairly young myself, when I crossed over, and it's an adjustment; I give you that. But you're not doing anyone any favors by enlightening them. We all have our place in the universe; as individuals and as a species. There are certain things I know that maybe I wish I didn't. Don't burden your mother with those things; not if you care about her."

Charlie could feel a deep ache in the pit of his gut. "What makes you think I don't care about my mother?"

"I'm not saying you don't. I'm saying the laws are in place for a reason. Knowing more than we were meant to know is dangerous; it can destroy us. Not so long ago, things were shared that shouldn't have been, and many paid the price." Phil shifted in his seat, "As far as how you feel about her, that's my gift. I don't move objects; I'm an empath. I can tell the two of you don't really get along."

Charlie adjusted his grip on the wheel, his stomach twisting into knots. *How many gifts are there? How many people like us are there?* He could feel his desire to know more swelling by the second, despite his passenger's advice. "What do we call each other?" he limited himself to one query at a time, "Those of us who've been there?"

Phil shook his head, "You're not going to heed my warning are you… you gotta know, no matter what it costs you."

"Yeah, I gotta know," Charlie's anger rose within him.

"Ok, here it is. The Universe is a big place, and we're only a small part of it. The Angels came here many centuries ago, some time after we became sentient, or self aware. They have their finger in lots of worlds; some that live, some that die. Of course, to hear them tell it, they *are* doing us a favor, but that's not how I see it."

He cleared his throat, "There's no name for us. We're the bastard children of their cause. Forgotten Angels, torn between two worlds; we don't belong in either of them, period. And we aren't supposed to remember their world if we come back here. But some of us do, for one reason or another."

"Were you a Dark Angel?" Charlie's tone held a hint of animosity, his doubts about the other man's honesty obvious. "I mean, how do I know you're not on a mission to corrupt me somehow?"

Phillip smiled at his distrust, "You don't."

"Oh."

"Yeah, I guess you could say I'm here strictly out of the kindness of my heart. Your mother is very broken at the moment. You don't see it, because you're hurting as well," his throat grated again. "That's really the reason that I introduced myself. Although, my trip to the diner had been the work of a Light Angel; I've gotten so used to my little assignments, I don't even question them anymore."

"So you do a Summer Angel's bidding?"

"Hmmp," Phillip grunted, "I don't like to see it that way. I could have chosen not to intervene."

"Why did you butt in then, if you didn't have to?"

"I did it for her," the deep voice dropped almost to a whisper. "This is a dangerous time for her, Charlie. And for you. The more you know, the deeper in you get. At some point, you lose all hope of ever getting out," he sounded forlorn.

"Yeah, I got that feelin' myself when Keeper said this would be my greatest challenge."

"Keeper said?" Phil tossed out sharply. His voice grew shrill, "You spoke to Keeper - when?"

"The day my dad died," came an anxious reply, "He came to the hospital to see me."

"You... saw Keeper," disbelief dripped from his lips as a tingle of sheer terror crept up his spine. "Stop the car!" Phillip demanded loudly.

"What? Why? You can't get out here! We're in the middle o' nowhere!"

"I can, and I am!" he unbuckled his seatbelt and reached for the latch.

"What the fuck, man? Let me at least get to a stop! An' what the hell's the matter with you!"

"You're already in over your head. If Keeper is actually paying you visits, there's nothing either of us can do to help you," he opened the door to climb out, "So I'll leave you with one last word of advice. Karma's a real bitch, Charlie. Stay on her good side." Without waiting for a reply, the tall slender man closed the door behind him and strutted down the road towards the diner they had left behind.

THIRTY-SIX

Don't Even

"WHAT'S GOING ON?" Beth called from the back scat, jarred awake by the slamming door.

"He wanted out," Charlie shrugged, watching the dark figure scurry across the road in the mirror. "Wanna jump up here with me?"

Making the switch, she glanced at the man barely visible in the distance, "Is he crazy? We just came from there."

"Haha," her son teased, "I tol' you we shoulda left him."

"Funny," she snapped her belt into place while he pulled back out onto the road. Driving along in silence for a short while, he thought about what the other man had said to him; *Forgotten Angels, that's what they should call us.* Somehow, knowing he wasn't the only one comforted him.

"Mom," he stated out of the blue.

"Yeah, baby."

"Mom, I know you an' me don't get along. I can't even say that we ever did."

"I'm sorry about that, son."

"I know," he cut her off, "But please listen, ok? That doesn't mean that I don't care about you, because I do. I never know how to take you; the way you're always buggin' me. Nothing I ever do is good enough," he ended abruptly, realizing that's not really what he meant to say. When she didn't respond, he sighed loudly.

The pair rode in an edgy silence for several miles before he noticed the sniffles in the the darkness. "Are you crying?" he demanded loudly.

"Shut up, Charlie. So what if I'm crying! You think I like hearing how I screwed everything up?" her voice quavered.

"Hey, I never said you screwed everything up," he countered, "So don't even go there."

"Well, you might not have said it…" her voice trailed away.

Great; two stupid as hell conversations in one night.

"Charlie, I screwed up," she sobbed.

Jesus Christ. "Ok, so you wanna take the blame, that's fine. I don't really care. I want things to be better from here; that's all that I want. I saw how you an' dad were, after my accident, so I know it's possible, if you want it to be."

"I do, baby," she wiped at her eyes. "I really do. I know that I'm overly critical. When you were little, I used to work in an office. I told your daddy I was burnt out an' I wanted t' take a little time off."

"A decade is more than a little," he corrected.

"I know," she snapped, "But I couldn't bring myself t' go back. The ladies I worked with called me a bitch behind my back. One day I overheard them laughing at me. About my weight, an' how I thought my shit don' stink!" She huffed a few times to calm her nerves, "I didn't know how t' face people after that. An' I didn't know I was doin' the same thing to you… or your father."

"How could you not know, mom?"

She bit her lip, shame coloring her cheeks in the darkness, "I really didn't, baby. I could justify everything I did; everything that I said. I came from a super-critical home, where negativity was the norm. I guess I never got past that."

"Aunt Belinda's the same way."

"Yes, she is," his mother agreed. "An' your uncle is, too. We all got it, an' I don't want that for you."

Charlie reached over, searching for her hand. Locating the digits, he wrapped them with his, "Ok, we need a plan. From now on, we need a code word. Whenever you are being critical, I will say the word, an' then you will be able to change."

"I'll try, honey. What's the word?"

"Peanuts."

"Peanuts!" she burst out laughing, "Why that?"

"I dunno," he gave her a squeeze, "Other people won't know what we're talking about, an' it sounds kinda fun."

A smile remaining on her pudgy mouth, she nodded to herself, "All right, then. Charlie an' mom, workin' together."

A small grin teased his lips as lights glowed in the distance. "I guess we'll stop for the night, now that Mr. Wonderful is no longer with us."

"He was such a nice man."

"Yeah," Charlie agreed, drifting into the conversation they had shared while she slumbered. *I wonder what exactly being empathic entails.* He had his doubts about the man's motives, but unfortunately there wouldn't be any way for him to discover more. *Unless of course I meet more of the Forgotten Angels* his mouth twisted into a wry grin; *an' now that I know they're out there, I'll definitely be on the look out for some.*

THIRTY-SEVEN

What Goes Around

CLARISSE STARED down at her new seeker, a few hundred butterflies taking flight in her gut, "Thank you, Destiny."

"You are welcome, my child."

"I'm sorry that I made such a mess of things."

A soft tinkle of laughter filled the air, "You have done no such thing, Summer Angel. All things happen for a reason. You know that I am the champion of all the great and wonderful things that we may become."

"Yes, I know this. But if that is so, why did you allow me to return to the plane of the living? Charlie is in a bad spot with Gous, and he may suffer greatly for my choice."

"Charlie needed you, Clarisse. He needed you to awaken certain things within him. It is part of his path, and it was your part to play," the head of the Light Angels soothed.

"But a Dark Angel hunts him, and would not have if I had left him alone. I couldn't bear to watch his future unfold without me, so I have left him unprotected," the girl sighed.

"Then go to him, my child. Do what you must, and do not fret that another should stand by his side, for you will always hold a place in his heart."

"Yes," Clarisse agreed. "Yes, he will always love me; I know that he will."

Touching the screen on her small device, her features brightened at the discovery of his location, "Oh, Destiny, do you know where he is?"

"Of course," she smiled pleasantly, "He's searching for you."

Beaming, the girl closed her hand, and instantly stood on a beach. The warm, midday sun glinting on her fair hair, she altered her clothing to a more suitable set of shorts and a tank top in her typical white. Stepping through the sand and enjoying the feel of it between her toes, she made her way to the pair of figures lounging at the water's edge.

"Hey, mom!" Charlie called with a giggle, "Let's build a sand castle!"

"Sure," she agreed, adjusting her straw hat against the breeze. Grabbing their bag of supplies they had purchased on the way over, she turned it upside down. "I'm sure some of this will come in handy for that."

Pulling out a small shovel and claiming one of the buckets, he began to pack it with moist sand. "We haven't done this in years."

"Nope. Not since our last trip t' Corpus, I guess when you were about eight. I was still working back then, so it had t' be at least that long ago."

Walking in a slow circle around the couple, Clarisse found herself smiling down at them; *I don't recall their ever being this happy together.* It had always been Charlie's father that spent time doing things with him. Lifting her gaze, she swept the shoreline, searching for the man. Then, opening her palm, she flipped through a few screens before covering her mouth to stifle her cry.

Oh, no! she whimpered. *John's gone!* She had left Charlie before the event, and had been concerned with her own problems at the time. "He needed me, and I wasn't there," she sighed.

"No, you weren't," a deep voice replied.

"Gous! What are you doing here!" she shrieked.

"Following my new recruit," he sneered.

"Charlie will *never* be one of you! I swear it on all that I am," she seethed.

"Still fighting over the boy," Father interrupted their volley. "You can't both win," he turned to the girl, catching a few floating strands, "But you both may well lose."

Shifting his gaze, Gous squinted slightly, "You think so, old man? He's already dark. I've seen it in him. All he needs is a little push."

"There will be no pushing, minion," Clarisse stamped her foot into the soft earth.

"Easy, Summer Angel," Father warned, "Take care that you are not drawn into his trap. For I suspect that Charlie is not the one he intends to take."

"The two of you bore me," the Dark Angel quibbled, "Leave me to my work already."

Lifting her chin, Clarisse shifted her gaze to the pair working on their sculpture; *they seem so happy. So oblivious to what lies around them.* A sad notion entered her mind, and she took a deep breath to hold her voice steady, "Is that true, Gous? Is it really me you're after?"

"Oh, my dear, it has always been you."

Avoiding looking at Father, she sighed, "If I were to pledge myself to you, would he then be set free?"

"Clarisse, you cannot do such a thing!" the elder spoke his piece.

"Father, I know this is a difficult decision. But if it would mean Charlie's freedom, I feel compelled to take such a path," she replied in a small voice. Hearing the Dark Angel's laughter, she shifted anxiously. "It is not for any other reason that I would allow such a thing."

"Then you must tell Charlie of this plan. I know the two of you have been communicating across the plane, as we did while you were on the other side."

Her eyes grew wide as she finally met his stare, "It was you! You left the message in the flour!"

"Yes," he admitted quietly, "I was the bearer of that unwelcome bit of news. It had to be, Clarisse, as this must also be done. Inform the boy of your decision, and hear what he has to say."

"Yes, Father," she agreed with a small nod. "I'll do it tonight," she glanced at her nemesis, noting that his expression had altered, and he no longer smiled. "You may still get your way, minion. Away with you, until tomorrow. Give us this one night of peace."

"As you wish," he acquiesced, "For soon you will be mine for eternity." Dropping his hood into place, he disappeared, leaving the two Summer Angels to observe their charges alone.

THIRTY-EIGHT

Escaping Fate

BETHANY LEANED back on her haunches to examine their creation. "This is really awful, Charlie," her laughter softened the blow.

"I know," he chuckled along with her. "I keep puttin' this one piece on there, but it refuses to stay. I feel like someone's kickin' my sandcastle!" he teased. Plunking another bucket of packed grains into position, he leaned back, his smile slowly fading; *holy shit. Someone is kicking my sandcastle.*

His eyes darting around wildly, his heart pounded heavily against his ribs. *What if it's her? Or even worse, what if it's Gous?* "Mom, I'm really tired. Maybe we should get over to the hotel an' get ready for dinner," he suggested quietly.

"I guess we can do that," she agreed half-heartedly. Getting to her feet, she patted him on the shoulder, "I had a really good time today, son. Thank you."

Blinking rapidly, he watched her put on her cover up and search for her flip flops, admitting a little more loudly, "Me, too. Maybe we can come back tomorrow."

"Sure. Or we could go apartment hunting."

Charlie's mouth fell open, "Apartment hunting! Why on earth would we do that?"

"Well, I've been thinking. You know they say everything happens for a reason," she paused, giving him a smile. "I wanna move," she finished by getting to the point.

"Oh, wow!" it felt like he'd been kicked in the gut. "That's a big decision, you know? I mean, dad just died, what, a week ago? An' you wanna pick up and move halfway across the country? You don't even know anyone here."

"I know, son," she picked up the bag she'd been packing and headed towards the car.

Hoisting the other tote, Charlie ran to catch up with her. "We'll talk about it over dinner," he puffed while opening the trunk.

Cutting her eyes over at him, she sighed loudly, knowing she should have kept the idea to herself, at least for a bit longer. Climbing into the passenger seat, they covered the few blocks to the hotel in no time, and she gathered her things to put on after she had washed up. "You mind if I have a long soak?"

"Naw, not at all," he grinned anxiously, still not sure what he could do about her crazy notion. Watching her disappear and close the door behind her, he flipped open his suitcase and yanked out the baking sheet. Sprinkling the powder lightly, he placed the canister on the table next to it with a thud, causing a small amount to form a cloud above it. "Ok, baby, are you here?"

A moment later, a smiley face appeared.

"Oh my God," he sniffled, overcome with joy to the point of tears. "I'm so happy you're back! I was so scared I'd never find you again."

I'm here.

"Are you gonna follow me around again? I don't really care if you do, baby. I really don't; but you can't interfere. Please don't take it the wrong way. I still love you, but I need some room, too," he begged as he swept the slate clean.

Gous is after you.

"I know," he breathed, "Or I suspected as much. He sent some guy to talk to me, an' I'm pretty sure he was a Dark Angel."

Clarisse stood next to the young man, longing to touch him. Instead she traced another message; *I have a plan.*

"Oh, that's great! What is it?"

Her eyes growing misty, she bit her bottom lip. *If I pledge myself to him, you'll be safe.*

Charlie felt crushed. "You can't do that!" he cried loudly, then recalled his mother still occupied the next room. "Seriously, Clarisse, promise me you'll never willingly belong to him! He's a horrible, vile creature! You'd be nothing to him; nothing but a possession, like a sofa," *or a dog;* Phil's words unexpectedly sprang to mind. "Oh, God!"

His eyes bouncing around the room, he wondered why he could see Keeper, but not Clarisse. *But, I saw her before, years ago.* What was different then? "You were a person before, right? A living being," he swiped the board.

Yes.

"What about Keeper? Was he ever a person?"

The girl stood gaping at him for a moment, relieved he could not see her shocked expression. She had no idea what to tell him, as this was a tender subject, and one not discussed by anyone who wanted to avoid being devoured by their highest superior.

He's an Angel, she finally scrawled.

"Ah, yes he is," Charlie sighed, "But where did he come from?" After what seemed an eternity, he realized she had no reply, maybe by lack of knowledge, but more than likely by choice. "It's ok," he finally breathed, "You don't have to answer that. I think I know. You can't pledge yourself to Gous. Not for me; it won't help, even if you do."

Why not?

"Because," he hesitated, swiping the powder, and then playing with it for a moment. "Because I'm special, Clarisse. In a way that you either can't see, or refuse to admit. They aren't gonna leave me alone. What-ever thing is going on over there, in that plane, it involves me. It's like my destiny; or maybe it's my fate. Either way, I can't escape it."

Oh, no, Charlie!

"Yeah; I figured you'd say that."

"Say what?" a voice called from the other side of the room.

Standing up straight, he swiped the tray clean, "Mom! Did you have a nice bath?"

"Sure," she agreed, using a towel on her hair, while inching closer to him, "But who were you talking to? I could hear you... so don' lie to me."

Charlie stared at her, the color draining from his face. His Adam's apple bobbed up and down, and he flashed her a quick grin, "You didn't believe that I could talk to her, but I still feel like she's listening, you know?"

"Donna," Beth lifted her chin and put an end to the grooming.

"Yeah," he shrugged a single shoulder, "Donna. So just let me grieve in my own way, ok?"

"Ok, then I need a pan, too."

"A pan?" he grimaced, his fingers dipping into the fine coating, "What for?"

"So I can talk t' your father," she quipped.

His laughter started low, making its escape as a low gurgle. Eventually building to a loud rumble, he countered, "Ok, so dad's an angel now; all right!"

"It's not funny, Charlie," she bit angrily. "Why can't he be, if Donna is?"

His smile slowly fading, the thought occurred to him, *what if he is?* An instant later, he suspected that would be impossible. *There's still way too much to this I don't understand,* but he knew enough to realize it was no accident that Clarisse had become a Summer Angel. *It's got more to do with it than being rifted,* he sighed. "I'm sorry, mom," he wafted his hand over his pan.

"I was only pulling your leg... about the magic," he lowered his chin in a sign of submission. "I was so... torn up, about losing her. I just wanted something I could cling to. If she's here, I'm still waiting for the sign."

"You talk to her like she can hear you," her bottom lip quivered, "And pretend like she's talking back."

"Yeah," he agreed. "Pretty stupid, huh?"

"No baby," she reached for her only son, "I don' think it's stupid at all."

Pulling her to him in a firm embrace, he knew he had to protect her from whatever came their way. *She's all I have left; I have to make sure she makes it through unscathed.*

THIRTY-NINE

Defining Dark Angel

CHARLIE AWOKE to the sound of the ocean. Lying in the darkness, he listened to the distant surf. Rolling onto his side, he stared at the curve of his mother's body beneath her blanket in the dim light. *I can't let anything happen to her.* He owed it to his father, as well as himself, to protect her.

Throwing back the blanket to his bed, he tiptoed quietly into the smaller room and closed the door. Flicking on the light, he unleashed the spray and climbed beneath the warm cascade. A clearer understanding had come to him while he slept, in the form of another dream about his time on the other side. *The darkness is coming, Summer Angel, and there is nothing you can do to stop it.*

That's the warning Gous had given to Clarisse. "Yeah, he's right about that," he spoke aloud in a hushed voice. "The question is, what are we gonna do about it?" He wasn't sure if she had joined him in the shower, but the idea of it brought a small smile to his lips as he recalled the love they had made while she lived in human form. *She'll be mine again;* one day, when they had put the world in order, he would make it happen.

Switching off the water, he used a towel to dry his tanned flesh, observing his new warm glow. *Wow, one day in the sun, an' I'm bronzed like a greek god,* he chuckled. As his thoughts turned, the smile faded, *oh crap! Things were revealed, and many paid the price.* Surely he didn't mean that literally. *But what if he did?*

Exiting the room, Charlie located his jeans and pulled them on over his cotton briefs. While he dressed, his mother interrupted his thoughts, "Wha's the plan today, baby?"

"I need to do a few things," he called to her quietly, buckling his belt and searching for a shirt. "Get some more sleep, an' I'll be back in time for lunch. Then we'll talk about your new apartment," he cajoled.

Smiling up at him, Beth felt a warm wave of joy flow over her, "You think I could pull it off?"

"Maybe," he leaned over her to kiss her forehead. "I'll be back soon." Carrying his canvas sneakers, he headed out the door to put them on in the elevator. *Now, where to look.*

His first thought was to locate Phillip Parson. *Of course, he took off as soon as he found out Keeper had come to see me.* That in itself held significance. *Whatever's going on with me is major.* That let Phil out, as he wouldn't willingly help. *Maybe I can locate someone else.*

I could get another set up, an' talk to Clarisse, he rationalized while exiting the front doors. Making a beeline for the beach, he sighed, *but she doesn't really know enough to help me.* He had begun to suspect her lack of knowledge had been a significant factor in the chain of events. *She's been kept in the dark, whether she knows it or not.*

Arriving at the boardwalk, he noticed a small cafe serving breakfast, and made his way inside. Taking a seat, he ordered coffee and a bagel with cream cheese spread. Facing the front glass, he could see the waves in the distance, and grinned to himself. *Clarisse loves the ocean,* he sighed, even though it had taken her life twice, more or less.

While he sipped his dark rich brew, a few more patrons came in, followed by two men who appeared over-dressed in their fluffy jackets. Observing the pair, the hairs on the back of his neck stood on end. Their eyes darting around the small room, they seemed to be preparing for something.

In a flash, Charlie leapt from his seat when one of them pulled a handgun from beneath his outer covering. Catching him off guard, he successfully knocked the weapon from his hand, while the other used his to crack the young man on the back of the skull, and a shot rang out. Chaos erupted around them at the sound.

Some of the patrons fell to the floor, crawling under tables and screaming. Others fled through the front door, calling for help, and two immediately began to film the fiasco with their cellphones. Shaking off the injury, Charlie got to his feet, his blood beginning to boil.

Lost in his anger, the boy fought back, the only way he knew how. Grabbing a metal napkin holder, he used it to bash his assailant in the face, sending the man reeling. Catching him by the chest, he struck him again, putting him on the ground.

Straddling his victim, Charlie raised his hand time and again, bringing the misshapen box down with the very force of his being, his blows more damaging than his arm alone could ever have been. Using his power, he channeled it through the object, pounding the flesh into oblivion.

The sound of the cracking bones of a human skull filled the air, and the second assailant used a chair to knock Charlie off of his friend. Rolling over, he stumbled to his feet, while others in their dining party subdued him and the would-be robbers. Forced to kneel on the floor, the young man placed his hands behind his head and waited, watching the blood pool around the lifeless body of the man he had beaten.

When the police arrived, Charlie and the second were cuffed and placed in the back of separate cars, while the first was loaded into an ambulance. His pulse slowed, his mind and body ached at what had happened. *I killed him,* he sobbed to himself, allowing the tears to trickle down his cheeks. *Is this what it's like to become a Dark Angel?*

The idea stuck in his mind, his thoughts ran in circles as he envisioned himself in prison. *Who's gonna take care of mom?* By the time they arrived at the station, he felt defeated and ready to accept whatever punishment was handed down to him. *Well, she wanted to live here; now she can visit me behind bars.*

Leading him to a small room, one of the uniformed officers removed his cuffs and instructed him to sit. Taking a seat at the table, he lay his arms across it, placing his face against the cool laminate until another gentleman in a suit joined him.

"Charlie?" he spoke in a calm voice. Seeing the young man lift his head, he nodded somberly, "I'm detective Barns. Rough morning, huh?"

"Yeah," the young man wiped at his damp cheeks, "Crazy seems to be following me lately."

"Is there someone we need to call for you?"

"Yeah, actually there is," he stretched, his mind blank for a moment. Giving him the name of their hotel, he said simply, "My mom was asleep when I left, so someone will need to take care of her."

Detective Barns smiled, "We'll send someone over," and he handed a note to the officer to his right, "Ok, son, I need you to fill me in on what happened at the shop."

Charlie shrugged. "I went in an' ordered breakfast; coffee an' a bagel. Then two guys came in and pulled out guns. I jumped one of them, and the other one smacked me in the back of the head for my effort. An' I lost it…" his voice trailed away, and he glanced around at the two other men who still shared their space.

"I grabbed the closest thing to me, an' I used it on him," he pounded his right fist into his left hand to illustrate. "I couldn' stop. I could hear the sound of the crunching," a tear trickled down his cheek, "An' I could see the blood goin' everywhere, but I couldn't stop hitting him. Then I got knocked off, an' a bunch of people jumped me. That's it."

He looked around, avoiding their eyes for a moment, then stared at his hands, "Is he dead?"

"He's bad," Barns didn't sugar coat it. "You from out of town?"

"Yeah, I'm from Texas. I'm a student in Austin," Charlie exhaled loudly. "I'm here on vacation with my mom."

The Detective rubbed his chin, "Any chance of you hanging around for a few weeks for us?"

Charlie smirked, "Well, that's ironic. Mom was talkin' about looking for an apartment, yesterday," he shrugged, showing the man across from him his palms, "We lost my dad… couple o' weeks ago. She said she might like t' move out here," he grinned. "I guess this makes it official."

"I guess it does. We're going to have you sign some papers, and you will need to provide me with your whereabouts," he stood and moved to the door, "And Charlie?" he called over his shoulder, turning on his way out, "Don't leave town."

FORTY

Secrets and Lies

"YOU THINK IT'LL WORK?" Charlie called to his mother from the second bedroom.

"Yeah, I think it's great!" she replied, the joy in her voice obvious. Joining him in the smaller of the sleeping quarters, she slid her arms around his waist, "Don't worry, son. We'll get through this together."

"I know," he dropped his arm around her back. The man he had attacked had passed away the night following his interrogation, leaving Charlie with an ominous feeling in the pit of his gut. The victim had tested positive for drugs, as had his companion, and that had added strength to his case. "It'll work out," he gave her a pat before he pulled away.

"So, we need to get things packed and ready to move," he ploughed on, "I filled out the paperwork over at the college yesterday, an' I think the transfer will be easy enough. I made straight A's last year, so if I don' get in, it won't be because o' my GPA," he chuckled.

"You'll get in," she grinned, her fingers trailing the counter in the small kitchen. "This's a new start for us."

"Yeah," he agreed. "Ok, so you take care of the paperwork, an' I'm gonna take a walk on our new beach," he indicated the stretch of sand across the street with a stiff thumb.

"Sure, baby. I'll come down there when I'm done."

Watching the traffic, Charlie made his way to the soft sand, pulling his shoes off at the edge so he could feel the warmth of it beneath his bare feet. Heaving a sigh, he dropped to his knees at the water's edge, then leaned over into a more reclined position. "Ok, Clarisse, where'd you go?"

He had been unable to reach the girl after his encounter with the police, and he feared that she had carried out her plan and had bound herself to Gous. *Maybe his attack on me through the robbery had been enough to push her over the edge.* Squinting into the brightness of the afternoon glare, he gave a startled jolt when a flowing brown robe suddenly appeared next to him.

Leaping to his feet, he breathed, "Keeper!"

"Hello, Charlie," the ancient being acknowledged him.

Dusting the granules from his clothes and grabbing his shoes, he followed the taller man along the beach, the water washing up enough to wet their feet. "Do you know where Clarisse is? I have t' know what's happened to her," he gasped hurriedly.

"Clarisse is in my care," Keeper replied calmly. "Interesting that your first concern is for her," he glanced at the younger man, "When so much in your life is unsettled."

"She's my soulmate," Charlie replied flatly. "What does that mean exactly, in your care?"

"I've given her a timeout; she and Gous both," he shook his head slowly, "Their fighting over you has gotten out of hand. Maybe after they have calmed down a bit, I will release them. That remains to be seen." He stopped to face the water. "For the time being, you need to work on you, Charlie."

"Work on me," the young man replied absently, a chill dancing up his spine, despite the heat of the day, "You make it sound like I'm under construction."

"You are," the bronze figure turned to him. "Everyone is, from the moment they are born. Although, some reach greater accomplishments than others."

"Yeah, about that," Charlie kicked the sand, "What if I don't wanna reach greatness? What if I jus' wanna be… normal."

Keeper chuckled, moving down the beach once more in his slow, ambling pace. "Charlie, you never cease to amaze me."

"Huh," he grunted, "So you have no real answer. You go on then. Keep your secrets and tell me your lies. I'll figure all this out, you mark my words, old man."

Stopping abruptly, the golden lips parted into a sneer, "Brazen; I don't recall the last time anyone spoke to me with such reckless abandon."

"They're scared of you; I'm not."

"Well," he chuckled, "I don't really know what to make of that, Charlie. Of course, you're young. You have a great deal to learn. Fortunately, you have a few hundred years to figure it out." Pulling his hands from behind his back, he clasped them in front of his elegant form, "I'll leave you for now, my son. Go on, discover what you can. But be careful. I don't want you getting into any more trouble, understand?"

"Yes, sir. I believe that I do," he gave the greatest of angels a small nod, and an instant later he stood alone. Glancing around at the few closest to him, he realized he had been alone all along.

Trudging along, lost in thought, his mind turned, *I need to find more of my kind; Forgotten Angels.* People who had seen the other side; people who retained their gifts. Spying his mother in the distance, he waved. *Here I thought I would eventually bring this whole adventure to a close,* he sighed to himself. *But it seems the story has only begun.* And with Clarisse in time out, he realized he would be walking his new path on his own.

Summer Spirit Series
Angels at War
Karma's Domain
Keeper of Worlds

About the Author

Anyone who knows me could tell you, I am a friendly kind of person, never met a stranger and take up conversations anywhere at any time. I work hard, and my mind never seems to shut down, as I wake up often in the middle of the night with ideas pouring out and demanding to be dealt with. Of course that means much of my books were written in the middle of the night.

I grew up and still live in the great state of Texas where everything is bigger, where we have warm weather and a central location. I love my state, my town, and my family, which includes my four sons, my significant other, and many friends as well.

I have thoroughly enjoyed writing this story and hope that you will love reading it just as much. And of course, there will be many more adventures to come.

You can follow Samantha Jacobey at:
Website: www.SamJacobey.com
Facebook: https://www.facebook.com/SamJacobey
Twitter: https://twitter.com/SamJacobey
Pinterest: http://www.pinterest.com/samanthajacobey/

Other works by Samantha Jacobey

https://www.lavishpublishing.com/authors/samantha-jacobey/

A New Life Series – an epic adventure, TORI FARRELL's life IS one wild story... escaped from a biker gang and running from drug lords... used by the FBI and hoping to protect her present from her past... IT'S DARK - IT'S BRUTAL, and it's WORTH EVERY MINUTE OF IT!! (Mature read, 18+ for graphic sexual content and violence, including rape)

Summer Spirit Series - no one EVER had a summer romance like this... Charlie visits another plane, parallel to our own, where Summer Angels and Dark Angels battle over the fate of man. A unique twist on an old idea that will keep you guessing; will Charlie and Clarisse ever find their HEA? (New adult)

Irrevocable Series – Armageddon through the eyes of an entitled seventeen-year- old, BAILEY DEWITT's life has become a broken mess... after her parents died unexpectedly, she didn't think it could get any worse. But when the arrogance of man catches up and puts the entire world into a dooms-day spiral, there will be only one place she can run to

- the one place she wanted desperately to escape. Can she and Caleb build a life together when the world is falling apart? (New Adult)

Teach Me to Prey – in this standalone thriller, JASON TRUITT and his friends have gotten their way for years. Deceit, sex, and foul play aren't normally covered in the curriculum, but they're doing whatever it takes to get under BECKY STEWART's skin. When one of the boys turns up dead, it's a race against time to save the others; a STUNNING STORY that will get your heart racing and leave you breathless by the end... (New Adult)

The Wicked Awakened – a Halloween novel; a five-hundred-year-old witch wants to turn SARAH MATTHEWS' body into her new home... A twisted tale involving a coven hell bent on seeing that she succeeds. Who will come out on top in this epic battle of wills? (Mature read, 18+ for graphic sexual content and violence)

The Binding - One cursed diary will change two strangers forever...Can Meri and Rider use her mother's old book to figure out why someone is after them? Or will the guilty party succeed, ripping the tome away before killing them and then slithering back into the darkness... (New Adult)

Sweet Christmas Series - Life isn't always sweet, even for girls called Candy. Candice Parker's life has never been easy. Plagued by losses and setbacks, each day is a struggle for the petite brunette and her young son. When fireman Gary enters her world, he is one mistake she refuses to make; but after tragedy strikes, she may not have a choice. (New Adult)

Also from the Lavish Publishing family

The Norn Novellas

A. Nicky Hjort

https://www.lavishpublishing.com/authors/nicky-hjort-1/

The Norn Novellas are all chapters in the epic saga of the youngest and most fickle of the four Norn Sisters. The same feisty immortal creature who must escape her inherent inner darkness to learn the meaning of life.

Each story takes a classic fairytale and spins it on its head, as we learn that maybe Norse Mythology was so much more than legend. And to think, you thought you knew those old tales so well.

Meet Za and find out what really happened...

Fairfield Corners
L.A. Remenicky
https://www.lavishpublishing.com/authors/l-a-remenicky/

Small town romance with a paranormal twist! Each in standalone style, read and enjoy any order, any number!

Saving Cassie – Book 1: Some secrets are too dangerous to keep.

After ten years in the big city, Cassie Holt is back in Fairfield Corners. She may look like the same girl who left home a decade before but she's hiding a dark truth from everyone. When her life is threatened by the demons of her past, her best friend—who happens to be the local sheriff—offers his help.

Deputy Logan Miller has been burned by love. He's not looking to get involved but duty calls when the sheriff tasks him with Cassie's protection. Thrown into close quarters with the gorgeous bookseller, sparks fly. Logan is drawn to Cassie, but it's hard to get close to someone who keeps themselves guarded all the time.

To keep Cassie safe, Logan must open his heart but that's something he swore he'd never do.

Ragan's Song – Book 2: One look into his eyes told her she was in trouble – again!

Ragan returned home to celebrate her parent's anniversary hoping they would forgive her the secrets she's kept from them over the last few years. When she discovered that Adam was still living in Fairfield Corners she hoped her secrets were safe, secrets that drove her away three years, secrets that could change both their lives forever.

Adam Bricklin was devastated when Ragan Newlin left town. No note, no email, no text. She was just gone. It has taken three years for Adam to finally move past the heartbreak he suffered when Ragan left town. Now he's moved on and everything was going well until the day Ragan returned to Fairfield Corners. Now the melody that he lost all those years ago is back. It's the same tune he heard that tells him right from wrong—the one that sang Ragan was the one.

Even separation can't silence Adam and Ragan's song, and now that she's back it's time for Adam to decide if he should let the song die or breathe life into it once again.

Where There's Faith – Book 3: A past she can't remember. A love he can't forget.

After losing everything in an accident that he can only blame himself for, Robbie Newlin embraced sobriety and tried to live his life quietly alone at this family's cottage on the lake. Grief being his only ally, Robbie was perfectly content with how he lived until Faith moved into the cottage next door. Now Faith had him questioning whether to keep grieving or to open his broken heart to let love in again.

Faith McMillan had no memory of her life before that day three years ago. The physical scars had faded but the emotional ones were still fresh and raw. Living rent-free seemed like a great way to finish her second book and give her the time to figure out her next move, but then she met the reclusive guy next door and everything changed.

To get past the broken parts, Robbie and Faith must figure out if they want to continue living their lives in solitude or take a chance on finding an ending together.